Princess Ponies

A Magical Friend
A Dream Come True
The Special Secret

The Princess Ponies series

A Magical Friend
A Dream Come True
The Special Secret
A Unicorn Adventure!
An Amazing Rescue
Best Friends Forever!
A Special Surprise
A Singing Star

Princess Ponies Bind-up:
A Magical Friend, *A Dream Come True*,
and *The Special Secret*

Princess Ponies Bind-up:
A Unicorn Adventure!, *An Amazing Rescue*,
and *Best Friends Forever!*

Princess Ponies

A Magical Friend

A Dream Come True

The Special Secret

CHLOE RYDER

BLOOMSBURY

NEW YORK LONDON OXFORD NEW DELHI SYDNEY

A Magical Friend, *A Dream Come True*, and *The Special Secret* first published in Great Britain in 2013
by Bloomsbury Publishing Plc
Published in the United States of America in 2014 by Bloomsbury Children's Books
Bind-up published in the United States of America in May 2017 by Bloomsbury Children's Books
www.bloomsbury.com

Bloomsbury is a registered trademark of Bloomsbury Publishing Plc

For information about permission to reproduce selections from this book, write to
Permissions, Bloomsbury Children's Books, 1385 Broadway, New York, New York 10018
Bloomsbury books may be purchased for business or promotional use. For information on bulk
purchases please contact Macmillan Corporate and Premium Sales Department at
specialmarkets@macmillan.com

Library of Congress Catalog-in-Publishing Data
for each title is available upon request
A Magical Friend LCCN: 2013034318
A Dream Come True LCCN: 2013036241
The Special Secret LCCN: 2013048653

ISBN 978-1-68119-494-3 (bind-up)

Typeset by Hewer Text UK Ltd., Edinburgh
Printed and bound in the U.S.A. by Berryville Graphics Inc., Berryville, Virginia
2 4 6 8 10 9 7 5 3

All papers used by Bloomsbury Publishing, Inc., are natural, recyclable products
made from wood grown in well-managed forests. The manufacturing processes
conform to the environmental regulations of the country of origin.

With special thanks to Julie Sykes

The Special Secret
For Sidonie, a true pony lover

The Pony

Queen
Moonshine

Princess
Crystal

Princess
Cloud

Princess
Stardust

Princess
Honey

Royal Family

King
Firestar

Prince
Jet

Prince
Comet

Prince
Storm

Chevalia

Horseshoe Hills

Savannah

Grasslands

Canter's Prep School

The Fields

Mane Street

Early one morning, just before dawn, two ponies stood in an ancient court-yard, looking sadly at a stone wall.

"In all my life this wall has never been empty. I can't believe that the horse-shoes have been taken—and just before Midsummer Day too," said the stallion.

He was a handsome animal—a copper-colored pony, with strong legs and bright eyes, dressed in a royal red sash.

The mare was a dainty yet majestic palomino with a golden coat and a pure white tail that fell to the ground like a waterfall.

She whinnied softly. "We don't have much time to find them all."

With growing sadness the two ponies watched the night fade away and the sun rise. When the first ray of sunlight spread into the courtyard it lit up the wall, showing the imprints where the golden horseshoes should have been hanging.

"Midsummer Day is the longest day of the year," said the stallion quietly. "It's the time when our ancient horseshoes must renew their magical energy. If the horseshoes are still missing in eight days, then by nightfall on the

3

eighth day, their magic will fade and our beautiful island will be no more."

Sighing heavily, he touched his nose to his queen's.

"Only a miracle can save us now," he said.

The queen dipped her head, the diamonds on her crown sparkling in the early morning light.

"Have faith," she said gently. "I sense that a miracle is coming."

Princess Ponies

Ponies

A Magical Friend

Chapter 1

Pippa MacDonald turned her pony, Snowdrop, toward the last jump, a solid-looking red-and-white wall. Snowdrop pricked up her ears. She snorted with excitement and sped up.

"Steady, girl," Pippa said, pulling gently on the reins.

None of the other riders had jumped a clean round. Pippa and Snowdrop were the last to go, and if they cleared the wall they would win the competition, taking home a silver cup and a blue ribbon. As the wall came closer, Pippa forced back the nervous, fluttery feeling growing in her stomach.

"We can do this," she whispered to Snowdrop.

She leaned forward, standing up in her stirrups, loosening the reins as she pushed her pony to the jump. Snowdrop leaped over it eagerly, carrying Pippa upward. For a magical moment it felt like they were flying. Any fear of heights simply slipped away. Fresh air rushed at Pippa's face, lifting her dark, wavy hair that was neatly held in place by a hairnet. Snowdrop cleared the wall, happily flicking her tail as she landed.

"Yes!" Pippa shouted, galloping Snowdrop over the finish line.

The crowd cheered and screamed, but one voice shouted louder than the rest.

"Pippa! Are you awake? It's time to go."

Pippa jolted out of her dream, nearly falling off her bed as Snowdrop, the show jumping arena, and the cheering crowds vanished. She blinked and stared around the small bedroom she shared with her big sister, Miranda.

It was easy to see which side of the room was Pippa's. Her wall was totally covered with pictures of ponies—big ones, small ones, black, brown, chestnut, roan, palomino, gray. Pippa's favorite picture of all was of Snowdrop, a silver-colored pony with deep-brown eyes.

Miranda's side used to have horse pictures too, but it was now covered with posters of boys—some were famous movie stars but most were in bands. Both sisters thought the other one's decorations were silly.

"Are you ready, sweetheart?" Mom asked from the doorway.

"Almost!" Pippa called, jumping off the bed and following her mom downstairs. "Did you remember to pack my bathing suit?"

"Of course," Mom said, smiling. "Now go get ready!"

It was boiling hot and Pippa was glad that she, her mom, Miranda, and their little brother, Jack, were going on vacation, trading their apartment in the city for a cottage by the sea. Pippa was so excited she trotted up and down the pavement, riding an imaginary pony as she waited for Mom to unlock the car so that they could load the luggage into the trunk.

"You're so immature," Miranda said, rolling her eyes as she climbed into the front seat.

Mom snapped Jack into his car seat and Pippa took her usual seat in the back, beside her brother.

"We're off!" cheered Pippa as Mom started the engine.

Dreamily, Pippa stared out the window, watching the busy city streets change to green fields filled with horses, cows, and sheep, until at last they arrived at their vacation home.

"Wow! Is it all ours?" Pippa exclaimed, as Mom pulled up in front of a small, white cottage surrounded by a huge yard. "I could have a pony if we lived here."

"Yes, the yard's big enough!" Mom

agreed, digging in her handbag for the key to the front door.

The cottage was right by the water. Pippa breathed deeply, loving the smell of the fresh, salty air.

"Can we go to the beach?" she asked.

Mom laughed at her impatience. "Let's unpack the car first. If we're going to the beach, you'll want to take your buckets and shovels."

"I'll help," Pippa said, pulling her bag from the trunk.

The cottage was even prettier inside. Pippa loved the attic bedroom, even though she had to share it with Miranda. It had sloping walls and a sea view, and, to Pippa's delight, there was an old horseshoe nailed to one of the roof beams.

"Horseshoes are lucky," she said happily.

Pippa skipped down the stairs into the kitchen, where Mom was searching their luggage for the bag of food.

"We'll have our lunch on the beach," she said, packing sandwiches, cupcakes, apples, and drinks into a picnic basket.

☆

The gate at the back of the yard opened onto a winding path that led down to the sea. Pippa was too excited to walk. Instead she galloped down the path, pretending to be a wild stallion, until she reached a horseshoe-shaped cove. Pippa stared in wonder at the golden sand and sparkling blue water stretching away from her.

The cove felt so secret and special it made Pippa's insides buzz with excitement.

"It's magic," she whispered softly.

Pulling off her sandals, she ran across the powdery sand to the sea, where tiny, white-crested waves were licking the shore. Just as Pippa was about to paddle in the water, she saw something far away. What was that at the mouth of the cove?

Pippa stared in amazement at two animals splashing in the water. "They look just like seahorses!" she gasped.

Pippa raised her arm to shield her eyes from the sun so she could take a better look. They really did look like seahorses, and they were almost as big as real horses, with gracefully curved necks bobbing above the water and long spines sticking up along spiky manes. One horse was pale pink and the other was green with dark freckles. Pippa blinked and rubbed her eyes. Was she imagining things? When she looked again the two animals were still there, splashing water at each other with their curled tails.

Behind her Pippa could hear Mom, Miranda, and Jack laughing together as they made their way to the beach.

"Quick!" she called, waving at them. "Look at this!"

"What is it, sweetheart?"

"Seahorses," Pippa said.

"Where? I can't see them!" Jack cried.

"Seahorses!" Miranda exclaimed.

"How can you see a tiny seahorse from here?"

"They're giant ones," Pippa said.

"I can't see anything." Mom stared out at the sea.

Miranda giggled as she ran over. "I see them! The red one's wearing a hat!"

Pippa's heart leaped, then sank right down to her bare toes. Miranda was teasing her! Besides, the sea was empty now. The seahorses had disappeared.

"I did see two seahorses," Pippa insisted. "They were playing together."

"Don't be silly, Pip. There's no such thing as a giant seahorse," Miranda said meanly.

"Pippa, you're too big for that sort of

make-believe," Mom said gently. "Come and help me set out the picnic."

Pippa gazed at the sea, but there was nothing there except for the sea-gulls gliding over the bay. But the seahorses *were* real—Pippa knew she hadn't imagined them. Confused, she hurried after Mom.

"Do I have to eat now?" she asked. "I want to go in the water first."

"Go ahead," Mom said. "Be careful. Don't go in deeper than your knees."

Pippa ran back to the water's edge. The sea was lovely and warm. She waded out until she was knee deep. The water was so clear she could still see her feet. Pippa wiggled her toes in the sand.

"Ooooh," she said. "That tickles!"

Two tiny seahorses were swimming around her feet.

"Wow! This place is full of seahorses!"

Pippa bent down for a closer look.

The moment her fingers touched the water they began to tingle. The feeling was so incredible that Pippa felt sure it was some kind of magic. Gently, she moved her fingers to get one of the seahorses to swim to her hand. The tiny animal was almost there when, suddenly, with a loud *whoosh*, the water rose up in the shape of the head and front legs of a galloping horse.

"Eek!" Pippa squealed.

Two giant seahorses popped through

the water and examined Pippa with their big eyes.

"You *are* real!" she exclaimed. "I knew I hadn't imagined it."

Pippa waded closer to the giant creatures and gently stroked their noses.

"Your name, Pippa, is short for Philippa, which means *lover of ponies*," said the pink seahorse.

"That's right," said Pippa, who couldn't believe she was talking to a giant seahorse.

"Then you are the one," said the green seahorse.

"My name is Rosella," the pink seahorse continued. "And this is Triton. We've come to take you to a place that needs your help."

With a flick of her pink tail, Rosella scooped Pippa up, placing her gently on her back. Then both seahorses surged forward through the foamy water.

"Where are we going?" Pippa asked.

"To Chevalia!"

Chapter 2

Pippa could not believe that she was riding a giant seahorse far out to sea. Rosella swam on, diving in and out of the waves, as Pippa clung to her gracefully arched neck. In a strange way, it was like riding a pony. Pippa stared at the delicate ears and long spines sticking out from the animal's neck.

Triton, the great green seahorse, was swimming next to her.

"Are you comfortable?" he asked kindly.

His voice was soft and deep, and it stopped Pippa from feeling scared. For a moment she was too speechless to answer.

"Yes, thank you," she whispered at last. "Are you taking me back to my mom? She'll be worrying like crazy."

Both seahorses chuckled.

"We're taking you somewhere very special, where time exists in a bubble," explained Rosella in a gentle voice. "You can stay there as long as you like and you won't be missed, for time will not pass in your own world."

"Where is it?" asked Pippa, her voice shaking with excitement.

"The island of Chevalia," said the seahorses.

Pippa looked out to the horizon and saw a large island surrounded by a long sandy beach.

"Wow!"

Pippa stared at the island in amazement. It was the most beautiful place she'd ever seen. So many questions were bubbling inside her, but before she could ask anything more, Rosella tipped her into the water and nudged her gently ashore.

"Chevalia is in danger, but you can help save it," said Rosella.

"Me? But how?"

"That is your quest," said Triton.

"Good luck, Pippa, lover of ponies," called Rosella.

She dived under the water with Triton and they swam away.

Pippa scrambled to her feet. She was standing on a sandy beach by the edge of a forest. At first it was very quiet. The only sound was the soft hiss of the waves gently lapping the shore.

Suddenly she heard a low drumming. Squinting into the sun, she saw a pony galloping toward her along the beach. Its long tail streamed out like a banner, and golden sand sprayed up from its hooves. Pippa's heart was racing. Who was this coming to meet her?

With a snort of surprise, the pony pulled up, sliding to a stop a few feet from Pippa. It was pure white and wore a tiara covered in sparkling pink diamonds. The pony's dark-brown eyes shone with excitement.

"A girl!" Reaching out, the pony touched Pippa with a velvety nose. "A real live girl!"

Pippa stared back.

"Y-you . . . you can talk?" she

stuttered. Pippa couldn't take her eyes off her. She was the most beautiful pony she'd ever seen.

"Of course," said the pony, tossing her head. "All ponies can talk, but only special humans can hear us. I'm Princess Stardust, seventh foal of the queen and king of Chevalia. What's your name?"

"Pippa," she answered. "I'm the . . . second child . . . of the MacDonald family . . . of Burlington Terrace."

"Have you been sent to help us?" Stardust's voice trembled.

"Help you?" repeated Pippa.

"To find the missing horseshoes," said Stardust impatiently. "If the eight magical horseshoes aren't found and returned to the Whispering Wall by sundown on Midsummer Day, then Chevalia will be lost forever. Quick! Jump on my back. I'll take you to the castle to meet my mother and father."

Excitement and fear fizzled through Pippa. She was on a secret island with talking ponies and she was going to meet the queen and king! She'd only ridden a few times—and never bare-back. But here in Chevalia, anything seemed possible. Pushing aside her fears, she jumped onto Stardust's back.

"Hold on to my mane!" called Stardust.

As Pippa sank her hands into Star-dust's silky mane, the pony spun around

and galloped across the beach toward the trees.

"We'll cut through the Wild Forest," Stardust neighed. "It's off limits, but it's the quickest way home."

Pippa could see eight tall towers rising above the treetops. The towers disappeared as Stardust entered the Wild Forest. Pippa shivered as the dark woods swallowed them too.

Chapter 3

There were lots of ponies in the forest, all with tangled manes and dirty coats. They were playing chasing games and having so much fun Pippa almost wished that there was time to stop and meet them. But Stardust thundered on, dodging bramble bushes and jumping over fallen trees. Pippa sat firmly, gripping with her knees and ducking to avoid the low-hanging branches. The

Wild Forest was on the side of a hill and as it grew steeper, Stardust slowed. She was breathing noisily and her sides were heaving.

"Stardust, stop and let me walk," Pippa called out.

"It's too dangerous for you," panted Stardust. "The forest is filled with quicksand that would swallow you whole."

Pippa gulped. She didn't like the idea of being eaten by sand.

"But don't worry," added Stardust. "I know the way!"

A little while later, the woods began to thin. Stardust sped up as they broke through the trees and came out on the edge of a large field. On the opposite side of the Wild Forest was a range of hills. To the right, at the other end of the field, Pippa saw a wide road, a collection of buildings, and a riding ring, where a group of ponies was gathered. Stardust started to gallop across the field toward the hills, when one of the ponies, waddling on stubby legs, noticed her.

"Princess Stardust! Come here at once!" she bellowed.

Stardust pretended not to hear, until the pony broke away from the group and galloped after them.

"Oh, horseflies!" Stardust exclaimed, pulling up and waiting.

"Who is it?" Pippa asked curiously, as the stocky brown pony hurried toward them.

Stardust rolled her eyes. "Mrs. Steeplechase, our nanny. She's just taken my brothers and sisters to school. I should be there too."

Mrs. Steeplechase stopped in front of Stardust, her nostrils flaring angrily.

"What do you think you are doing? The Wild Forest is *strictly* off limits."

"Sorry," Stardust apologized. "I thought school had been canceled because of the emergency. I was looking for the missing horseshoes, but instead I found Pippa. She's been sent to help us. Isn't that fantastic?"

Suddenly Mrs. Steeplechase noticed Pippa.

"A human girl!" she snorted with alarm. "And what's she doing riding on your back as if you were just any old pony? Get down, girl. You can walk the rest of the way."

"But——" said Stardust.

"Don't argue," said Mrs. Steeplechase fiercely. "She might be dangerous. What will Queen Moonshine and King Firestar say about this? A girl indeed!"

Pippa's heart sank. She hoped that the king and queen weren't as unfriendly as the royal nanny. She turned pink with embarrassment and slid down from Stardust's back.

"Don't mind Mrs. Steeplechase—she's all whinny and no kick. Mom and Dad will be thrilled to see you," Stardust whispered. She began to mimic Mrs. Steeplechase, walking stiffly after her, copying the way Mrs. Steeplechase's large bottom swung from side to side.

Giggling quietly, Pippa followed Stardust over the field and along a winding path. After a while, the path opened out at the top of a hill. Pippa stopped and stared.

Ahead of her, between the other hills, was Stableside Castle, the biggest castle she'd ever seen. Its white stone walls sparkled like pearls in the bright sunlight. Eight flags, each a different color but all decorated with a golden horseshoe, fluttered from the tall towers, and the enormous wooden drawbridge was lowered, as if to welcome them.

"That's my tower," Stardust said, pointing her nose at the smallest one, which was topped by a pink flag, waving in the breeze. "It's got the best view in the whole castle."

A group of horses was standing by the drawbridge with cameras around their necks, obviously waiting for someone to come or go.

Mrs. Steeplechase shook her head. "The ponarazzi are still here then! We'll have to take the secret path and go in through the back way, or else the girl's picture will be all over the island by tomorrow."

"They're always trying to take pictures of the Royal Family," said Stardust.

"No talking and hurry up," Mrs. Steeplechase said sternly, as she trotted down the hill toward a small door hidden in the castle's walls.

Pippa felt butterflies in her stomach as she followed behind Mrs. Steeplechase. Stardust's hooves crunched on the white gravel at the base of the castle wall, and Mrs. Steeplechase turned to Stardust.

"Try to trot quietly, child," she said.

But Stardust ignored her nanny and continued to clatter beside her. She did not seem worried that she was in trouble.

The hidden door led into a large courtyard with a stage on one side, and a huge stone wall behind it. The wall was bare except for eight imprints of horseshoes. Stardust blinked back a tear.

"That's where the golden horseshoes should hang," she whispered.

A wave of sadness hit Pippa and she had to catch her breath. She glanced around and saw piles of silk ribbons and flowers on the ground. It was as if the courtyard had been abandoned suddenly. A small chestnut pony was sweeping them up. A trail of black hoof-prints led to the door they'd come in. Pippa stared at the hoofprints. Something about them bothered her, but she couldn't quite put her finger on it.

"We were decorating the castle for the Midsummer Ball," Stardust said, nodding at the ribbons. "But now no one has the heart to get things ready. It's only a week away and it takes forever to prepare everything, especially the food for the banquet."

Mrs. Steeplechase trotted across the courtyard to a wooden door guarded by a black pony wearing a red sash. The pony bowed his head, then nudged open the door.

"This is the Royal Court," Stardust

whispered, as they entered a large room full of perfectly groomed ponies with gleaming coats and polished hooves.

One by one they fell silent, staring at Pippa with wide eyes as she walked across the room. Pippa felt very small as she made her way nervously through the crowd. All the ponies wore brightly

colored sashes, some decorated with jewels. A chestnut pony with big eyes, a square nose, and emeralds in her mane gave Pippa a very mean look. Next to her, a smaller pony with the same shaped nose and eyes gave her an identical hard stare.

"That's Baroness Divine and her daughter Cinders," whispered Stardust. "No one likes them. They think they're so much better than anyone else. Cinders shouldn't even be here. She should be at school, like me."

Mrs. Steeplechase stopped in front of a beautiful palomino pony with a long white mane and tail, and a large copper-colored pony. Stiffly, she bent one leg, bowing her head to the ground. Stardust copied, leaving Pippa standing awkwardly between them. Unsure what to do, Pippa curtsied as if she was greeting her ballet teacher.

"Your Majesties," said Mrs. Steeplechase, rising slowly. "Princess Stardust has found a stranger on our island. A human."

"So I can see," said the queen, her brown eyes resting on Pippa. "What is your name, child? And where do you come from?"

Suddenly Pippa felt very shy. She stuttered her name.

"P-P-Pippa MacDonald. From Burlington Terrace."

"Isn't it wonderful!" said Stardust. "Pippa's been sent to help us find the missing horseshoes."

All the ponies in the room began

to whisper. Baroness Divine stepped forward.

"No human has ever set foot on Chevalia before. How can we trust her?" she demanded.

"She's a pony lover," said Stardust angrily. "Only a true pony lover can find Chevalia and understand our language."

Queen Moonshine stared at Pippa, making her squirm inside, but she stood tall, hoping the queen would see that she had nothing to hide.

"Chevalia is a very special place. It needs horse and pony lovers from around the world to keep it alive," the queen said in a low voice. "Their love is captured by the eight magical horseshoes that hang on the Whispering

Wall. Once a year, the magic in those horseshoes must be renewed by the Midsummer sun or it will fade. If that happens, then our beautiful island will sink into the sea."

Pippa gulped. Now she understood why Princess Stardust was so sad that the wall was bare.

"This is a time of great danger," Baroness Divine said. "Midsummer Day will be here soon but the magical horse-shoes have disappeared. How did you get here? Who told you that Chevalia needed help? How do we know we can trust you?"

Chapter 4

The Royal Court was so quiet that Pippa was sure everyone would hear her heart thudding.

"I didn't know Chevalia needed my help," she answered truthfully. "I was on vacation with my family when a magic wave scooped me up. Rosella and Triton brought me here."

The ponies stared at Pippa in awe. An excited murmur rippled around the regal room.

"The human girl saw Rosella and Triton—but why? They never show themselves to humans," a pony said.

The queen stamped a hoof for silence.

"There is an old legend that tells of a human girl who comes to Chevalia in its time of need. The seahorses brought you here, so I believe you are that girl." She touched Pippa on the top of her head with her muzzle. "Welcome to Chevalia. Good luck with your quest. If there is anything you need, then please ask."

"She needs me," Stardust said, trotting forward.

Mrs. Steeplechase frowned.

"Hush," she scolded. "You may only speak to the queen when she speaks to you."

"But Pippa is *my* pet! I found her. Besides, how else will she find her way around the island?" Stardust insisted.

The queen tried not to smile.

"I'm sure we can find Pippa a good guide," she answered. "Perhaps your big sister Crystal——"

"I'd really like Stardust to help me," Pippa said bravely, interrupting the queen.

The queen looked uncertain.

"Let Stardust help," the king said. "It will be good for her to have some responsibility for a change."

"Very well," said the queen. "You'd better start right away. Time is running out."

"Thanks, Mom," whinnied Stardust.

"Your Majesty," she added quickly, when Mrs. Steeplechase glared at her.

As Stardust and Pippa left the court, Cinders started complaining.

"It's not fair," she whispered loudly, so that Pippa could hear. "Princess Stardust gets everything. I want a girl too. I've wanted one much longer than she has."

"Hush," said the baroness. "Better things come to those who wait."

"What does she mean?" asked Pippa.

"Don't pay any attention to her—she's always been jealous of the Royal Family," said Stardust. "Come on. Let's start searching for the missing horseshoes."

Stardust used the same hidden door they'd entered the castle by.

"Where are we going first?" asked Pippa.

"Mane Street," said Stardust. "It's where everyone hangs out."

"It doesn't sound like a very good hiding place," Pippa said doubtfully.

"Exactly!" said Stardust. "If I were hiding something, that's where I'd put it, because no one would think to look there. Hop on my back. It's so much fun when we gallop together."

"But what about Mrs. Steeplechase?" asked Pippa.

"Horseflies to Mrs. Steeplechase! Mom and Dad didn't tell you not to ride me, did they?"

Pippa didn't need a second invitation. She loved riding Stardust, and her mouth stretched into a wide grin as she jumped onto her back.

☆

Mane Street was the wide, grassy road on the field that they had crossed earlier.

"That's my school," Stardust said proudly, as they passed Canter's Prep School for Fine Equine. "Miss Huckleby is the best teacher ever. You should hear her read *Black Beauty*."

Stardust's school was a blue wooden building with window boxes overflowing with colorful flowers and tubs filled with carrot sprouts.

"The carrots are for snacking on," Stardust said, pulling up two and giving one to Pippa.

Crunching on their carrots, they

peered in through the windows, where a class of ponies was starting a math lesson.

Stardust giggled.

"Look at Honey admiring her sparkly hoof polish. She's my third-oldest sister. The grumpy-looking pony wearing the boring wooden tiara with the acorns is Cloud, my second-oldest sister. My

oldest sister is Crystal. She's left Canter's now. She's going to be queen one day, and she never lets us forget it!"

Cloud turned to the window with a scowl, and Stardust quickly pulled Pippa away.

"Don't let her see you," she said. "She'd want to know why I'm not in school, and there isn't time to explain."

They crept around the back of the school, passing the riding ring Pippa had seen earlier, and a green field where some tiny ponies were learning to trot. Stardust barely glanced their way, but Pippa held back, sure she saw something shining in the long grass at the edge of the field. Could it be one of the missing golden horseshoes? She hurried over and was disappointed to find it was just an ordinary old horseshoe.

Pippa's eyes grew wider and wider as Stardust pranced along Mane Street pointing out all her favorite stores. Pippa noticed that all the shoppers were staring back at her too!

"That's the salon where I go to have my mane and tail washed. They have gorgeous strawberry-scented shampoo. And look—Dolly's Tea Rooms. You should taste their buckets of hot carrot juice. Delicious!" Stardust said, smacking her lips. "And there's Mr. Gem's. He sells the nicest jewels ever."

It reminded Pippa of the main street back at home, only Mane Street was much prettier, with beds of sunflowers decorating the sidewalks and tiny silver horseshoes strung from the old-fashioned streetlights. Everything was spotlessly clean—even the silver water troughs had been polished until they shone. The street was packed with ponies, and Pippa was amazed to see so many different types. There were well-groomed ponies, stocky working ones, and scruffy little Shetlands. Everyone seemed very quiet, mostly talking in whispers. When a pony whinnied with laughter, the others frowned.

"It's been like this since the horse-shoes went missing," sighed Stardust.

Pippa was beginning to doubt that they'd find any of the golden horseshoes here. There were too many ponies and

not enough hiding places. There was an amusement park at the end of the street, though. That looked like a more promising place to hide things.

"Should we look in there?" she asked.

"That's where I'm taking you!" Stardust said excitedly. "You should see the merry-go-round. It's rainbow-colored with tiny flashing lights. It's so pretty. And the ghost train is really scary. It's even got Night Mares."

"Night Mares?" asked Pippa. "What do you mean?"

"The Night Mares are spooky-looking ponies. They've lived here forever, even when Chevalia was just a tiny lump of volcanic rock and not the magical island it is today. I've never seen one, but

everyone says they're really mean." Stardust shivered. "Do you want a ride on the ghost train? It's a lot of fun."

"I thought we were looking for the horseshoes," said Pippa.

Stardust blushed.

"We are! It's just so wonderful having you here, and I want to show you everything. But you're right. Finding the horseshoes is the most important thing. Without them Chevalia will lose its magic."

Stardust shuddered, her brown eyes suddenly glistening with tears.

"Don't worry," Pippa said, stroking her neck. "I promise we'll find the horseshoes."

"Really?" Stardust sniffed. "Thank you, Pippa. You're the best pet ever."

Pippa opened her mouth to argue that she wasn't a pet, but Stardust was already heading into the amusement park.

The amusement park was less crowded than Mane Street. None of the ponies, except for the really young ones, seemed to be enjoying themselves.

Pippa and Stardust walked around the rides but found nothing.

"Let's search the rest of the fields," Stardust said finally. "They're big enough to hide all eight of the horseshoes."

Pippa and Stardust spent the rest of the day walking the fields. It was hard work and there were many false alarms. By late afternoon Pippa had met many of Stardust's friends, and they had both found lots of precious items that other young ponies had lost—like hair clips and combs—but they hadn't found any of the golden horseshoes.

As the sun began to set, they made their way back to the castle. Pippa was hungry and very frustrated that they

hadn't discovered any clues about where the missing horseshoes might be.

"We both need a hoof massage with dandelion hoof balm," Stardust said longingly, as they passed the Mane Street Salon. "But Mrs. Steeplechase is very strict about mealtimes. She won't let us go out together tomorrow if we're late."

"We *must* find those magical horse-shoes tomorrow," said Pippa.

Meals were eaten in a huge dining room with three stone feeding troughs, and a special gold one at the front of the room for the queen and king. Everyone stared at Pippa as she followed Stardust to a trough.

As the serving ponies carried in buckets of steaming oats and mashed carrots, Pippa wondered what she was going to eat, but she didn't need to worry. One of the cooks came out of the kitchen to serve her personally.

"Chicken fingers and fries!" Pippa cried delightedly. "My favorite!"

There was even a knife and fork to

eat with. As Pippa began to eat, Stardust watched in amazement.

"So that's what those are for!" she exclaimed. "I've only ever seen them in the Museum of Human Artifacts."

Pippa laughed, and listened to the ponies whinnying around her. Most of their chatter was about the missing horseshoes. Pippa caught her own name several times and a few of the ponies shyly nodded at her. But not everyone was as friendly. Several refused to look, turning away if Pippa smiled at them. She finished her meal with a rosy red apple. It felt good to eat after such a busy day.

When Stardust and Pippa left the dining room to go to bed, one pony neighed at them as they passed.

"It's funny how the girl arrived at the same time that the horseshoes disappeared. I don't trust her."

The words stung, but Pippa held her head up high. The ponies of Chevalia needed her, and she wasn't going to let them down.

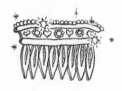

Chapter 5

Stardust's room was right at the top of the eighth tower of the castle. Instead of stairs, there was a spiral ramp. It was large and round, with curved stone walls. On her dressing table, in a special place, was a little doll that had washed up on shore.

"I've wanted a girl ever since I was a foal, but I never dreamed I'd get one," Stardust explained.

"I've wanted a pony forever too," said Pippa.

Stardust looked confused but then she laughed.

"I get it! You're my pet and I'm yours."

"Can't we just be friends?" Pippa asked.

"Friends," Stardust said slowly. "That sounds nice. Yes, let's be friends."

"You're a magical friend," said Pippa.

"No, you're a magical friend." Stardust laughed again.

Stardust slept in a huge bed with a straw blanket and a horseshoe-shaped headboard covered with ribbons. Pippa slept on a special cot next to her. The bed was surprisingly comfortable, and she fell asleep immediately.

☆

The next morning, Pippa woke up early.
Stardust was still snoring softly, so she
stared out of the window. Pippa was
terrified of heights and at first it made
her feel sick being so high up. Taking
deep breaths, she looked out over the
magical island. It calmed her to think
about all these ponies living together in
such a special place. She watched the
ponies strolling on Mane Street, and in
the distance she spotted ponies working in the fields. As she looked out to
the sea, she could see nothing around
for miles, and she reminded herself that
Chevalia would be lost if she didn't
keep her promise.

Pippa counted the days on her

fingers. There were only six left until Midsummer. Time was running out. They had to find the golden horseshoes before it was too late. Yesterday had been fun, but Pippa worried that Stardust had been more excited about touring Chevalia and showing off her new friend than she had been about searching for the missing horseshoes. Today would be different. Pippa decided it was time to take charge.

Anxious to get started, Pippa gently shook the pony awake.

"You're still here!" Stardust whinnied with delight as she opened her eyes. "I thought I might have dreamed you."

Quickly, she rolled out of bed and nuzzled Pippa's dark hair.

"Me too," said Pippa. "But it's not a dream, and we're going to find the missing horseshoes."

Stardust took a long time getting ready so Pippa helped, combing her mane and tail, to hurry her along.

"I've been wondering where to go today," Stardust said. "We could visit the Grasslands or the beaches. Or perhaps we should start with the Savannah, where the striped ponies roam wild. Then there's the Horseshoe Hills and the Volcano. Maybe not the Volcano—it's spooky there." Stardust shivered.

Pippa stopped combing as an idea clicked into place.

"The Volcano!" she exclaimed. "Maybe that would explain the black

hoof marks I saw in the courtyard yesterday. I wondered where they'd come from. Everywhere in Chevalia seems so clean, especially around the castle, but volcanoes are covered in ash."

"Are you sure?" Stardust asked uncertainly. "Wouldn't you rather search the beaches? We might find some clues there."

"But the black hoof marks are a clue!" Pippa said, her voice rising with excitement. "We *have* to search the Volcano."

"I'm not sure," Stardust said reluctantly. "Storm—he's my youngest brother—told me never to go there. It's too dangerous."

"Then I'll go on my own," Pippa said stubbornly.

Stardust's eyes widened.

"You'd really do that?"

Pippa nodded. She'd promised to save Chevalia and she would keep her word, no matter how dangerous it was.

"Then I'm coming with you," said Stardust.

Pippa hugged Stardust around the neck, pleased that she didn't have to go to the Volcano alone.

Even though she was nervous, Pippa was impatient to get started. After a quick breakfast of cereal and apples, she and Stardust went to the back door. It was very early and the door was still locked. Stardust pulled back the bolts with her teeth.

"Maybe the Night Mares stole our horseshoes," said Stardust. "Storm thinks that they live on the Volcano, but Comet, my bookworm brother, says that's just a myth. But if it was the Night Mares, then how did they get inside the castle? All the doors are locked from the inside at night."

"Maybe someone helped them," suggested Pippa.

"No!" Stardust exclaimed, sounding shocked. "Why would anyone do that?"

Pippa shrugged. She didn't know either. Chevalia was so special, she couldn't imagine anyone wanting to harm it.

Pippa could hardly believe how much her riding had improved in such a short time. She felt as comfortable riding Stardust bareback as if she'd been riding with a saddle. How impressed her pony-crazy friends back home would be if they could see her now!

At last, they entered the foothills,

staying on the path so that they didn't get lost. The higher they went, the steeper the path grew. Sometimes it ran alongside the cliff. Pippa didn't like that—it made her dizzy to look down and see the jagged rocks falling away beneath her. Stardust seemed to sense her fear and kept away from the edge.

It was very peaceful. The only sounds were the clopping of Stardust's hooves, the cry of the birds soaring overhead, and a soft rushing noise that Pippa couldn't figure out until they reached a small stream that crossed the path.

"So that's what I could hear," Pippa said, as Stardust jumped the stream then stopped for a drink.

"Try some," she said. "It's fresh and it's clean."

Pippa slid from Stardust's back and, kneeling down, scooped up the water in cupped hands. It was freezing cold and made her fingers tingle.

"Mmm, that's delicious," she said, enjoying a long drink.

Stardust nudged her playfully, her long white mane falling over Pippa's arm.

"That tickles!" Pippa giggled, nudging Stardust back.

Stardust dipped a hoof in the stream, splashing water at Pippa.

"Water fight!" she neighed.

"Water fight!" Pippa agreed, splashing Stardust back.

Stardust splashed with her hooves and Pippa with her feet. They both disappeared in a shower of water, which

sparkled like diamonds in the sunshine, until Pippa and Stardust were soaking wet.

"Stop!" Pippa begged, laughing, pushing her soggy curls away from her face.

"That was so much fun," Stardust whinnied, shaking herself dry and soaking Pippa all over again.

"Eeww!" squealed Pippa. "I didn't think I could get any wetter!"

It was already very hot, and as the friends climbed higher the sun soon dried Pippa's clothes. After a while, they followed another stream that snaked alongside the path before tumbling over a cliff in a fast-flowing waterfall.

"It's beautiful!" Pippa gasped.

"Chevalia is beautiful," Stardust said, her face clouding with worry. "I can't understand why the Night Mares would want to harm it."

"It might not have been them," said Pippa.

"Who else could it have been?" Stardust asked. "No one knows about

Chevalia. Only true pony lovers can see it, and a true pony lover would never harm us."

Pippa twisted a curl of her hair around her finger. "But the island's not going to disappear. We're going to find the golden horseshoes."

"Promise?" asked Stardust.

"Yes," said Pippa.

Knowing it was a sign of friendship in ponies, she leaned forward, softly blowing air at Stardust's nostrils.

Stardust blew air back.

"Thank you, Pippa," she whispered. "You're a true friend."

Pippa pushed away her worries as she smiled at Stardust. Promises were easy to make, but could she really keep hers?

Yes, she told herself firmly. She would not break her word. She *would* find the golden horseshoes in time to save Chevalia.

Chapter 6

As Pippa and Stardust neared the bottom of the Volcano, the path grew steeper. It was covered with black rocks.

"They're hot!" exclaimed Pippa. She picked one up and quickly put it down again, brushing the black dirt from her hands.

"Yes, and this is as far as we can go," Stardust said nervously. "I think the Night Mares live near here."

"So now we look for clues?" Pippa asked.

Stardust nodded.

"But only on this side of the Volcano. We can't stray into the Cloud Forest on the other side. No one's allowed to go there. Not even Mom and Dad."

"Why not?" asked Pippa.

"It's haunted," she whispered.

"Oh," Pippa said, feeling both scared and relieved.

The Volcano was so big it would have taken forever if they'd had to search it all. She hoped she wouldn't have to look for the horseshoes in a haunted forest.

Side by side, Pippa and Stardust started to hunt for clues. At first

Pippa was very excited, thinking that they might find all eight of the horse-shoes. The rocky landscape had lots of nooks and crannies, perfect for hiding things in. Each time she saw something shining in the sun Pippa rushed forward, and each time she was disappointed.

"I'm thirsty," Stardust said at last. Her white coat was smudged with dirt and her long tail was full of tangles. "Let's go back to the stream for a drink."

She was trotting toward the path when something soared overhead.

"What's that?" Pippa cried, pointing upward.

Stardust swung around.

"What?" she asked. "I can't see anything."

"It's gone." Pippa was dismayed.

"Maybe it was an eagle?" said Stardust.

Pippa fell silent. The thing she'd seen had been far too big to be an eagle. As she followed Stardust to the stream, the creature flew over again. Pippa's eyes widened.

"Look!" she shouted. "It's a flying horse!"

Stardust spun around again.

"Peggy!" she exclaimed.

Peggy had a silvery coat, a long mane and tail, and an enormous pair of feathery wings. She circled overhead, tilting slightly as she drifted through the air.

"She's amazing," Pippa breathed, her heart thudding. "Stardust, I think she's trying to tell us something!"

"I don't think so," said Stardust. "Peggy hardly ever shows herself—you're lucky to have seen her. I think she's curious about you."

Pippa shielded her eyes with her hands as she squinted at the flying horse.

"But look how she keeps dipping her wing. It's at the same place every time. And then she turns her head to see if we're watching her."

Stardust stared in silence.

"It might be nothing, but maybe we should check it out," she said at last.

Forgetting their thirst, Pippa and

Stardust hurried back the way they'd come. Peggy remained overhead, still flying in the same circle, until the friends were directly underneath her. Suddenly she swooped much lower, hovering right above a rocky ledge. Whinnying loudly, she reared up. Then, with a flick of her silvery tail, she flew away.

"Look!" Pippa said, breaking into a run. "There's something sparkly up there on the ledge."

Pippa and Stardust raced across the rocks until they reached the ledge that Peggy had shown them.

Stardust neighed with excitement.

"I can see something shining in the grass."

Pippa stood on tiptoe. In the middle of a clump of grass, something was shining with a soft yellow glow.

"It must be one of our golden horse-shoes!" she exclaimed.

The horseshoe was so well hidden that if it hadn't been for Peggy, Pippa and Stardust would never have spotted it. Nervously, Pippa rubbed her hands on her shorts. The ledge was more than twice her height and she'd have to climb it to reach the horseshoe. The thought made her feel hot and shaky. She couldn't do it. The ledge was much too high.

"Stand on my back," Stardust said eagerly.

Pippa had always been afraid of heights. She didn't move.

"Don't worry—you won't hurt me. I'm really strong," Stardust said, misunderstanding Pippa's reaction.

Pippa was still a little scared, but she jumped onto Stardust's back. She sat for a moment to work up the courage to keep going.

Come on, you can do this, she silently urged herself.

Slowly, Pippa stood up. Her heart was racing and her legs shook like a jellyfish. Stardust remained completely still, and slowly Pippa relaxed. That wasn't so bad! Now all she had to do was stretch up to grab the missing horseshoe. But frustratingly, it was just out of reach. Pippa stretched as far as she dared—any farther and she'd lose her balance.

"It's no good," she called at last. "I can't get it. Can you move any closer?"

"I'm as close as I can get," said Stardust.

Pippa stared at the ground and immediately wished she hadn't. Quickly, she sat back down, clinging on to

Stardust's mane until her head stopped swimming.

"Are you okay?" asked Stardust.

"I'm fine," Pippa replied, licking her dry lips.

She was going to have to dismount and climb up to the ledge instead. But as she slid down from Stardust's back, she saw a long, sturdy stick. Snatching it up, she waved it in relief.

"I might be able to reach the horse-shoe with this."

Being careful not to hit Stardust with the stick, Pippa scrambled onto her back once more. But as she reached up to hook the horseshoe, she froze. What was that? Above the ledge, to the right, was a large slab of rock, where two scruffy-looking ponies with thin, straggly manes and tails were arguing loudly. Pippa's insides turned to ice.

"They must be Night Mares!" she whispered.

Chapter 7

Pippa stayed still and listened to the Night Mares' argument.

"How did you manage to drop a horseshoe, Nightshade?" the smaller pony whinnied angrily. "The Mistress said to hide it carefully so that the Royal Ponies wouldn't find it! It just goes to show that even though you're bigger than me, you're not smarter."

"Be quiet, Eclipse. Nagging me isn't

going to help me get the horseshoe back," Nightshade whinnied.

"But how will we reach it from here?"

"Use that branch behind you."

As Eclipse turned to look at the branch, Pippa snapped into action. With trembling hands, she reached up to hook the golden horseshoe down from the ledge. It was very heavy, and although Pippa's stick was long enough to touch it, she couldn't drag the horseshoe toward her. Swallowing her frustration, she tried again.

"What's happening?" called Stardust. "Have you got it yet?"

"Shhh," whispered Pippa.

But it was too late.

"Who's that?" asked Nightshade. She

peered over the rock and her eyes locked with Pippa's. "Eclipse, it's a girl!" she neighed. "And she's stealing my horseshoe!"

"Prancing ponies!" cursed Eclipse.

Breathing heavily, Pippa blocked out Nightshade and Eclipse's frantic conversation and concentrated on getting the horseshoe. Using both hands to hold the stick, and hoping that Stardust wouldn't move a muscle, she dragged the horseshoe down. But Eclipse had also found a stick on the ground, and she was trying to pull the horseshoe up. It was turning into a tug of war! Eclipse's stick was larger than Pippa's, but the pony was holding it in her mouth and having trouble controlling it. Steadily, Pippa dragged the horseshoe to the edge of the ledge. As she reached out to pick it up, Eclipse brought her stick crashing down.

Just in time, Pippa snatched her hand out of the way. She sat down on

Stardust's back and tightly clutched the horseshoe.

"I've got it!" she said triumphantly.

"Hold on tight!" Stardust said, turning sharply to gallop back down the Volcano.

"That's *my* horseshoe!" Nightshade shouted after her.

As Stardust gathered speed, her hooves thumping on the ash-covered path, the Night Mares' voices faded away.

Pippa started to wonder who Eclipse had meant by "the Mistress." She clung on to Stardust, wrapping her free hand around the white mane and gripping with her knees. Stardust didn't stop until she was safely at the bottom of the Volcano, where she pulled up in the shade of a tree. Pippa slid down from her back and fanned her friend with a feathery green leaf. It was several minutes before Stardust caught her breath.

"We did it," Stardust said, trembling with excitement. "We found our first

horseshoe. I can't wait to show Mom and Dad. They'll be thrilled!"

Pippa's smile was so wide it almost reached her ears, but her stomach felt nervous. That had been so scary.

"So you were right—it *was* the Night Mares who stole the horseshoes!"

She hoped the other seven horseshoes would be easier to retrieve, but what if they couldn't find them?

"What do you think?" Stardust asked impatiently, pawing the ground with a hoof.

"Sorry, what did you say?" Pippa realized that she hadn't been listening.

"Nightshade and Eclipse think we've gone home," Stardust repeated. "We could sneak back and follow them.

They might say where the other horse-shoes are—or who this mysterious Mistress is."

Pippa slid the golden horseshoe into her pocket.

"I think we should take this one back to the castle first and hang it where it belongs. We don't want to lose it again."

Stardust sighed. Her new friend was very sensible.

"You're right. The horseshoe needs to be back on the wall so that it can pick up the love from all the horse and pony lovers around the world. It's what keeps Chevalia alive."

In silence, they hurried to the castle, entering by the back door and going straight to the Royal Court.

As the guard opened the large wooden door, Pippa pulled the horseshoe from her pocket and handed it to Stardust.

"You take this," she said.

"No way!" exclaimed Stardust. "You rescued it. You can give it to Mom and Dad."

The Royal Court was packed and noisy, but when the ponies saw the golden horseshoe they immediately fell silent. Pippa followed Stardust over to her parents.

Queen Moonshine's eyes lit up with joy.

"You've found one of our horseshoes!" she whinnied. "That's wonderful. I'm so proud of you both."

"This is fantastic," King Firestar agreed, stamping a large hoof. "And now the horseshoe must be put back where it belongs."

One of the court's helpers trotted over, but the king waved him away.

"Thank you, Conker, but I shall hang the horseshoe myself," he said.

Pippa was pleased—she didn't really want to hand over the missing horse-shoe to anyone other than the queen or the king.

A procession of horses followed them to the Whispering Wall, where King Firestar rehung the horseshoe. Stardust was so excited that she couldn't stand still, and she danced on the spot.

When the horseshoe was back in its

place, the crowd neighed loudly. But the single horseshoe looked very small and lonely hanging on the wall.

Pippa clapped, but part of her felt worried. There was still so much to do.

"Congratulations," Queen Moonshine said in a low voice. "But your quest has only just begun. Midsummer Day will soon be here and there are still seven horseshoes to find. Go safely, my children, and remember not to count your horseshoes until they're hung!"

"We won't, Your Majesty," Pippa said earnestly.

Both the queen's words and seeing the golden horseshoe hanging on the wall had filled her with a new confidence. They could do this. Together she and Stardust would find all the missing horseshoes.

"To Chevalia!" she cheered.

"To Chevalia!" Stardust echoed. "And to you, Pippa, my magical friend!"

Princess Ponies ♥

A Dream Come True

Chapter 1

Pippa MacDonald blinked sleepily and stared around the unfamiliar room. For a moment she didn't know where she was. She remembered going on vacation to the beach with her family, but this wasn't their vacation home. The bed next to hers was huge, with a straw blanket and a horseshoe-shaped headboard decorated with ribbons. And fast asleep in the big bed was a pony—a princess pony!

All at once Pippa's memory flooded back. She *had* been on vacation, until two enormous seahorses had whisked her away to the island of Chevalia, a magical world filled with talking ponies, where no human had ever set foot before. Time existed in a bubble there, and Pippa wouldn't be missed at home, for no time was passing in her own world.

There she'd met Princess Stardust, and learned that Chevalia was in great danger. Eight golden, magical horse-shoes used to hang on an ancient wall in the castle courtyard. Once a year, on Midsummer Day, the horseshoes' energy was renewed by the sun. But the horse-shoes were missing, and if they weren't returned by Midsummer Day, Chevalia would be gone.

Pippa had been amazed to learn that she'd been brought to Chevalia to find the magical horseshoes. Yesterday, after a long, exciting, and danger-ous search, she and her new friend, Princess Stardust, had rescued one horseshoe from the foothills of the spooky Volcano. But there were still seven more to find and there were only five days left until Midsummer.

Quickly, Pippa got up and looked for her clothes. She'd hung them on a chair the night before, but now in their place was a new outfit—a white top covered in pink and blue horseshoes, a pair of pink jodhpurs, and some matching sandals. Thrilled, Pippa put the new clothes on, then borrowed one of Stardust's combs to untangle her dark, wavy hair.

Stardust was still fast asleep.

"Wake up, lazy hooves," Pippa said, gently shaking her.

Princess Stardust opened her eyes, yawned, and closed them again.

"There's no time for sleeping in," said Pippa. "Chevalia is still in danger."

"I was having the most wonderful dream," mumbled Stardust. "I had a pet girl." Her eyes flew open and she sat up. "It was true!" she exclaimed. "I really do have a . . ."

Pippa scowled and crossed her arms over her chest.

"I mean, a new special friend," said Stardust hurriedly. "Today's a very special day—we should get ready."

Stardust went to her dressing table and combed her long, white mane. Then Pippa placed Stardust's pink jeweled tiara onto her head, between her ears. Pippa smiled

as she adjusted the sparkling tiara into place.

"Let's get going then," Stardust said excitedly.

Stardust's room was at the top of the eighth tower in Stableside Castle. They hurried down the tower's spiral ramp to the ground floor. They were just heading toward the dining room for breakfast when Stardust's big sister Princess Crystal appeared, going in the opposite direction.

Crystal had an apricot-colored coat with an inky-black mane and tail and a white blaze running down her face. She was extremely pretty and spent many hours making sure she looked her best.

"Hurry up," she whinnied impatiently. "There's a family meeting in the courtyard."

"A family meeting about what?" Pippa whispered to Stardust.

"We're always having family meetings," she said. "I'm starving—are you? What about breakfast?" she called after Crystal.

"You should have thought about that when you were sleeping in. It's a good thing you're not going to be queen one day." With that, Crystal trotted ahead, toward the courtyard.

Pippa put her hand on Stardust's side.

"Don't mind her," she said. "Big sisters just don't understand."

"She still treats me like I'm a foal," said Stardust.

"She may have a bigger tiara," Pippa said, smiling, "but you have a girl for a best friend."

"Yes, I do," Stardust said, smiling back and following her sister.

Reaching the wooden door that opened onto the courtyard, Crystal stopped and turned around. "It's Royal Family only," she said importantly. "Your pet should wait here."

"Pippa's my best friend and she's here to save Chevalia," said Stardust. "That makes her the same as family!"

Crystal rolled her eyes. "You make me tired," she neighed, leading the way.

Stardust and Pippa joined the Royal

Ponies gathered in the courtyard. Crystal and Prince Jet stood at attention, nudging each other for the best position to greet their mom and dad. Prince Comet had his nose buried in a book. Honey was doing twirls to show off her glittery new hoof polish, while Cloud was mumbling grumpily. Prince Storm strode in last, covered in mud, causing Crystal to snort angrily.

"Storm, you could have washed. You look like you just trotted off the farm!"

"I did," he replied. "The fields won't plow themselves."

"Stop bickering, children," scolded Mrs. Steeplechase, the royal nanny. She pushed the Royal Ponies into an orderly line, ready to welcome the king and

queen. "I trust you've all had breakfast and are ready for the Royal Games?"

Pippa's stomach rumbled noisily as she looked at Stardust in alarm.

"Games?" she asked. "But I thought we were going to search for the missing horseshoes."

"Was that your stomach, Princess Stardust?" Mrs. Steeplechase asked angrily. Dipping her head inside her satchel, she brought out a shiny red apple and tossed it to Stardust, who caught it in her mouth. She threw another apple to Pippa.

"Thank you," Stardust and Pippa said.

"Hmmph!" snorted Mrs. Steeplechase. "Just don't be late for breakfast again."

Pippa stared at the stone wall, where one lonely golden horseshoe sparkled in the sunlight. There were still seven empty spaces left to fill. Suddenly she didn't feel so hungry anymore.

Stardust followed Pippa's gaze to the Whispering Wall.

"The Royal Games are very important—" she started, but she was interrupted as the queen and king trotted regally into the courtyard.

As one, the Royal Ponies straightened up, with their ears held forward. Bowing their heads, they whinnied, "Good morning, Mother. Good morning, Father."

The queen looked up at the wall and then turned to address her children. "The annual Royal Games are taking place today, and although Chevalia is in danger, it's important that we keep up our traditions. The whole island will be looking to us for how to behave. If we panic about the missing horseshoes, then everyone will panic. Do you understand?"

The Royal Ponies nodded and chorused, "Yes, Mother."

"Stardust," Pippa whispered, "if the Royal Games are so important, maybe I should look for the horseshoes on my own."

"Don't do that," said Stardust. "You'll miss out on the fun. There are so many great events—dressage, show jumping, horseshoe-tossing, polo, and the

17

Equestriathon race around the entire island!"

"The Games do sound amazing," said Pippa.

"They take place on the Fields," explained Stardust, "on the far side of Mane Street. It's not too far from the beaches, so we can search them afterward."

"Okay," Pippa said, feeling a little happier that Stardust wasn't completely forgetting about the horseshoes. "We'll stick together."

"Like best friends," said Stardust.

"Like best friends," Pippa agreed, stroking Stardust's long, soft mane.

Queen Moonshine whispered something into her husband's ear, then turned and nodded at Pippa.

Pippa flushed and her stomach did a cartwheel. She could guess what the queen had said. The Royal Ponies and the ponies of Chevalia were depending on her.

"We *will* find the missing horse-shoes," Pippa said determinedly.

Chapter 2

Queen Moonshine lined her family up in age order. Princess Crystal was first, perfectly groomed and dressed in her best tiara, looking every bit the queen-in-training. She was followed by her three brothers and three sisters, with Stardust, the youngest Royal Pony, at the end.

"What a fuss," Storm said quietly. "I don't know why I have to go to the

Royal Games when there's so much to do on the farm before the harvest."

"But the polo team needs you," said Stardust. "You're their best player."

"Do you play polo, Stardust?" asked Pippa.

"I wish I could play, but Mrs. Steeplechase won't let me. She says I'm too young." She sighed. "The only game they let me play is horseshoe tossing, which is for babies."

The king and queen led the Royal Family from Stableside Castle to the Fields at a smart trot. Pippa was glad that Mrs. Steeplechase had allowed her to ride on Stardust's back or she might not have kept up. Pippa looked out for the missing horseshoes as she rode toward the

Royal Games grounds. Away to her left was the Wild Forest. She was surprised to see that three ponies were gathered by the edge of the trees. The largest, a stocky pony, was cloaked in a dark-gray coat and hood, with a few strands of chestnut mane showing. There was something familiar about it.

"Stardust," Pippa whispered urgently, "who's that over there by the Wild Forest?"

"Where?" asked Stardust.

"Right there," Pippa said, pointing. But when she looked again, the ponies had disappeared into the woods.

"Was it the wild ponies? They're lots of fun. I wish I was allowed to play with them," Stardust said.

Pippa fell silent. They hadn't looked like wild ponies and Pippa was sure she'd seen the large, hooded animal before. If only she could remember where.

As they approached the Royal Games grounds, the delicious smells of warm bran mash and steamed carrot juice drifted toward Pippa. An enormous horseshoe arch marked the entrance. It was decorated with red, blue, yellow, green, pink, and purple ribbons that fluttered colorfully in the light breeze. One by one, the Royal Family ducked under the horseshoe arch, to the excited hoof-stamping of the hundreds of

gathered ponies. The queen led them into the royal box, which was higher than the rest of the audience and gave an excellent view of the entire show ring.

Knowing that the whole crowd could see her, Pippa carefully slid off Stardust's back. There was a loud crackle followed by a shrill whinny, then a deep voice sounded over the loudspeaker.

"Ponies and foals, please show your appreciation for the arrival of Their Majesties Queen Moonshine, King Firestar, and the Prince and Princess Ponies: Crystal, Jet, Cloud, Honey, Comet, Storm, and—not forgetting the little foal of the family—Stardust. Plus our very special guest, Pippa MacDonald."

There was a thunderous roar and the ground shook with even more stamping. Pippa's face felt hot and her chest tightened as she stared shyly at the enormous crowd. She'd never seen so many ponies all in one place. There was every kind, from tiny Shetlands with shaggy manes covering their eyes to magnificent thoroughbreds with highly polished coats.

"Mmm, can you smell that carrot juice?" said Stardust. "I could drink a whole trough of it."

"You're only hungry because you slept through breakfast," Cloud said irritably.

"I could drink a troughful of carrot juice too," said Honey. "Let's go and get some together. Do you like my hooves by the way? I wasn't sure which color to paint them."

"I *love* your hooves," said Stardust.

"They are pretty," Pippa said, taking in Honey's glittery pink-and-purple-striped hooves.

"Where did you get the polish from?" asked Stardust.

"The Mane Street Salon. Excuse me!" Honey said angrily, as Crystal and Jet pushed past to get to the front of the royal box.

"Out of my way, Jet. The crowds are here to see me," said Crystal.

"No, they're not," Jet said, winking at a group of young fillies and grinning when they blushed. "It's me they're here for."

"Well, they're certainly not here for me," Storm said, smiling at Pippa.

"I'm not surprised," Crystal said moodily. "You might have cleaned up your hooves at least, Storm, before coming to stand in the royal box."

"Don't worry, Storm," Stardust whispered. "No one's interested in me either."

Pippa sighed. Stardust seemed to have forgotten they had an important job to do.

"I'm going to start looking for the horseshoes," Pippa said impatiently.

"Wait for me! Sorry, Honey, I've got to go," added Stardust. She hurried after Pippa, stepping out of the royal box and into the crowd.

"We'll never find anything here. There are too many ponies around!" Pippa worried. Then she thought of something. "Do you think the crowd would help us?"

"That's a great idea!" said Stardust.

Stardust's excitement was contagious, and she soon had a group of eager ponies helping her to search the show ground. Pippa tried asking for their help too, but most of the ponies just stared at her in awe. They had never seen a real live girl before. In the end she gave up asking and searched alone, keeping her head down to avoid all the curious stares.

The dressage competition started and many of the ponies lost interest in searching for the horseshoes and trotted over to the arena to watch. The Royal Family was settled in the royal box, enjoying the Games. Honey had a large bag of roasted nuts that Stardust kept looking at longingly.

"Let's go and watch the dressage for a bit," she said at last, when she couldn't resist any longer.

"We can't," said Pippa. "There are only five days left until Midsummer."

Stardust nuzzled her nose in Pippa's dark, wavy hair.

"I know," she said softly. "But you heard what Mom said about the Royal Ponies needing to act normally. Let's search for a bit longer and then we really have to go and watch some of the events."

Among the trees at the edge of the show ground was a temporary stable block for the competitors. It was packed with ponies combing their manes and painting their hooves. Sashes and tail bandages fluttered from the trees and there was a strong smell of hoof oil.

A flash of light caught Pippa's eye. It was coming from a hollow in a wizened old tree. Something shiny was hidden inside. Her heart quickened as she went toward the light and pulled out the shiny object.

"It's just a hoof pick," she said, her shoulders sagging with disappointment.

"That's my lucky hoof pick!" said an excited voice. "At least, I hope it's lucky."

Pippa turned around to see a solid, chestnut pony, with a neatly braided mane tied with blue ribbons, trotting up behind her.

"Blossom!" Stardust whinnied, blowing through her nostrils at the pony.

Blossom blew back, giggling as they touched noses.

"Are you competing in the junior dressage?" asked Stardust.

"I can't get out of it," Blossom said sadly. "You will come and watch me, won't you? Pleeeeease! I know I'll mess it all up if my best friend isn't there to cheer me on."

"I'll try," Stardust said. "But Pippa

and I are busy right now. Pippa's here to find the missing horseshoes and I'm helping her."

A hurt look crossed Blossom's face, but she swallowed and said bravely, "I know. Everyone's talking about her—a real live girl here on Chevalia."

"She's my best pet ever," Stardust said proudly.

Pippa rolled her eyes and cleared her throat, hoping that Stardust would remember that she wasn't a pet.

"I mean, Pippa's my best friend," Stardust said quickly, realizing her mistake.

Pippa noticed that Blossom's big brown eyes glittered with tears.

"B-b-best friend?" she stuttered. "I thought I was your best friend."

"You are. Well, you were until Pippa arrived," Stardust said. She did not see that Blossom was sad. "Pippa's my best friend now, but you can be my second best."

Just then the announcer called for the start of the junior dressage competition.

"Listen—they're calling your class," said Stardust. "You'd better go."

"So are you coming to watch me?"

"I'm sorry, Blossom, but Pippa and I—"

"We'd love to watch," Pippa interrupted. "We'll both cheer you on!"

Pippa felt very uncomfortable as

they followed Blossom to the competition arena. It was obvious to her that Blossom was upset, but Stardust didn't seem to have noticed.

"Blossom's too clumsy to be any good at dressage," Stardust whispered. "It's too bad, because she comes from a family of show ponies."

When it was Blossom's turn to perform, she trotted stiffly into the ring. Her hooves were all over the place and she kept tripping up.

Cinders, an unkind pony who was always quick to criticize others, was in the box below the royal one. She laughed as Blossom stumbled around the ring.

"Blossom's got four left hooves,"

she whinnied. Some of the other ponies laughed and snorted with her.

That only made Blossom worse. She trotted around the show arena like a circus clown. She finished with a shaky curtsy and hurried from the ring in tears.

"What's wrong with her?" asked Stardust. "She always does badly in dressage, so why is she crying about it now?"

"Blossom's crying because you said she wasn't your best friend anymore," Pippa said quietly.

"That's silly!" Stardust exclaimed. "We can still be friends, but how can I have two best ones?"

"Very easily," said Pippa. "It's good to

have lots of friends. Imagine how you'd feel if I suddenly said I wanted to be Blossom's best friend and not yours."

Stardust's face fell. "I thought you liked me!"

"I do, but that doesn't mean I can't like anyone else. I've got another best friend at home."

"But you like me at the same time?"

Pippa nodded.

"Oh, I see," Stardust said slowly. "You *can* have two best friends."

Now that the junior dressage was over, Pippa wanted to continue searching for the missing horseshoes but she didn't want Blossom to be so upset, especially when it was partly her fault. She decided to hide her impatience because she knew they had something to do first.

"Let's go find Blossom and tell her she can be your best friend too," Pippa said.

Stardust looked unsure. Pippa climbed onto her back and stroked Stardust's mane.

"Having two best friends will be twice as much fun," Pippa promised.

"Okay," said Stardust. "I will have two best friends. Let's go and tell Blossom."

Chapter 3

At first Stardust and Pippa couldn't find Blossom. They searched everywhere, including the competitors' area, but there was no trace of her. Then Stardust spotted her on the far edge of the show ground.

"Blossom's going the wrong way!" she said. "That path leads down to the beach."

"She's fast!" Pippa exclaimed, watching Blossom gallop into the distance.

Blossom galloped all the way down the path and didn't stop until she reached the beach. Stardust was hot and panting heavily by the time they caught up with her. Blossom stood staring out to sea with the surf swirling around her legs.

"Hi, Blossom," Stardust said breathlessly. "You can still be my best friend if you want. Pippa says I can have two."

Pippa slid from Stardust's back and glared at her. "Say sorry," she mouthed silently.

Stardust tossed her head as if she might argue, but Pippa kept glaring at her.

"I'm sorry," she said at last. "I didn't mean to hurt your feelings."

"Really?" Blossom continued to gaze at the sea.

"Yes," Stardust said, giving her a friendly nudge with her nose.

Finally, Blossom turned around. "So we're still friends?" she asked.

"*Best friends*," said Stardust. "It's going to be twice as much fun having two best friends."

"Can I be friends too?" Pippa asked, looking at Blossom.

"Yes! A real live girl for a friend would be amazing," said Blossom. "I'm sorry I ran away. I was upset, and when Cinders laughed at my awful dressage performance it was the last straw. I try so hard but I always trip over my hooves."

"You're great at galloping," Pippa said kindly. "You should enter the Equestriathon."

"I'd love to, but Mom and Dad think that racing is for any old pony, not show ponies like us." Blossom sighed.

"Traditionally Blossom's family has always been a family of prize show ponies on Chevalia," added Stardust.

"She can't just decide to be a racing pony."

"But we can't all be good at the same things," said Pippa. "My mom says you should do the things that make you happy."

"Well . . ." Blossom paused. "I do love to gallop—it's my favorite thing. Well, that and being Stardust's best friend."

"Pippa's right," said Stardust. "You should do the things that make you happy. And even if you don't win the trophy, every pony that finishes the race gets a medal. But I'm sure you *can* win!"

Blossom fell silent for a while, then she said bravely, "I'll do it. I'll race in the Equestriathon. And if I win the trophy, hopefully Mom and Dad will be so proud of me they won't mind about the dressage. Will you come and support me?"

"Of course," said Stardust.

Pippa bit back her frustration. She couldn't hurt Blossom's feelings by refusing, but she was worried that at this rate they'd never find the missing horseshoes.

"Thank you." Blossom's eyes sparkled happily. "And one more thing, now that we're all best friends—can Pippa ride me in the Equestriathon? Pleeeeease! You know how much I've always wanted to carry a girl."

"That's a great idea, isn't it, Pippa?" said Stardust.

Pippa hesitated. "Won't you run faster without me, though?" she asked.

Blossom's bottom lip quivered.

Pippa didn't like seeing her upset again, so she quickly added, "How about I just ride you to the start line?"

"That would be wonderful! Thank you, Pippa. We'd better get going. I need to warm up on the practice gallops."

As Blossom and Stardust trotted back up the beach, Pippa trailed behind, kicking up lumps of seaweed and check-ing behind rocks for the missing horseshoes.

When they reached the path toward the Fields, she turned back for one last look. Something caught her eye away in the distance. Pippa squinted out to sea and her heart missed a beat. It was Rosella and Triton, the two giant seahorses who had brought her to Chevalia. She wondered if they would be able to help. Pippa ran straight back to the water's edge, waving to get their attention. Gracefully, the seahorses changed direction and swam toward her.

"Hello, Pippa," the pink seahorse named Rosella called.

"Is there a problem?" asked Triton, a green seahorse with dark freckles.

"Yes," Pippa said breathlessly. "Princess Stardust and I have only found one of the golden horseshoes."

"Only one?" exclaimed Rosella. Pippa noticed that the seahorses gave each other disappointed looks.

"We brought you here, Pippa, because you are the girl who loves ponies the most," said Triton. "We hoped you could save Chevalia."

Pippa felt awful. "I won't let you down," she promised, "but I could use your help."

"What help do you need?" asked Rosella.

"Could you swim around the island and look at the places we can't see or reach from the land, like the rocks?"

"If there are horseshoes on the cliffs or in the rocks underwater, we'll find them," said Triton.

"Thank you," Pippa said gratefully.

Proudly dipping their heads, they swam back out to sea.

Pippa raced to catch up with Stardust and Blossom. The two ponies were so busy talking about how Blossom should compete in the Equestria-thon that they hadn't even noticed she'd been gone.

While Blossom warmed up for the race on the practice gallops, Pippa searched the ground on either side of the racetrack for horseshoes. She wasn't surprised when she didn't find them, though—it was too open and flat to hide anything there.

At last it was time to ride Blossom over to the Equestriathon start line on the beach. A long blue ribbon marked the start of the race and a huge crowd had gathered all along the track. As Blossom approached it, proudly carrying Pippa on her back, the ponies began to whisper and stare. Pippa's face burned with embarrassment when she realized they were talking about her.

"Carrying a girl is cheating," said a large pony with a narrow face.

"It's not fair to the others," agreed an elderly black-and-white pony.

Pippa was very glad when Blossom reached her position on the start line. Sliding from her back, she stood close to Stardust, hoping the princess pony could protect her from the mean looks. Once she was off Blossom's back,

everyone returned their attention to the competitors.

"Good luck, Blossom!" Stardust shouted, earning herself a glare from Mrs. Steeplechase, who was also in the crowd. "Once you've started, we'll go to the cliffs to watch the rest of the race."

"Thank you," Blossom said, looking pleased. "I couldn't do this alone."

King Firestar stepped forward. "One hoof, two hooves, GO!" he called, striking a horseshoe-shaped gong.

The blue start-line ribbon fell to the ground. In a thunder of hooves and flying turf, the competitors galloped away. Blossom kept pace with even the

biggest and most powerful of the racing ponies.

"Quick, Pippa," said Stardust. "Jump on my back so we can get to the cliffs faster. It's the best place to watch from because you can see at least half the race from there."

As soon as Pippa had swung herself

onto Stardust's back, the pony set off at a gallop across the Fields. The wind blew in Pippa's face, catching her wavy hair so that it streamed out behind her. She felt her worries slowly melt away. This was thrilling—the most fantastic ride in her whole life. She wanted to gallop forever. Leaning forward, she sank her hands deep in Stardust's soft, white mane.

"Faster," she cried.

Stardust snorted. "Hold on tight then," she called, pushing onward.

Pippa could tell that Stardust was enjoying the ride too. Her ears were pricked forward and she galloped with a joyous spring in her stride.

Pippa was so happy she almost

shouted out loud. She felt so alive—
and confident that everything would
work out. Blossom would win the race,
she was sure of it.

Chapter 4

They reached the cliffs quickly and Stardust stopped a safe distance from the edge, her sides heaving as she caught her breath.

Pippa looked around. From this point, over half the island's white beaches were spread out below her. The island was ringed by deep-blue water that sparkled like thousands of tiny jewels. It was so quiet up here that she could hear the soft hiss as the waves crept up the shore. But the beaches were a long way down and it gave her a sudden shiver to be up so high. She clung onto Stardust's mane and Stardust gently moved back, sensing Pippa's nervousness.

"That's much better," said Pippa. "Chevalia's the most beautiful island ever, but it's very, very high up in some places!"

Pippa looked down the stretch of beach to watch the ponies racing across the sand. Even though they were so tiny from this height, it was still possible to pick them out. White sand sprayed from their hooves as they thundered along. The stocky chestnut in the

lead was Blossom. In second place, and a long way behind, was a paint pony, his neck stretched and steam rising from his body as he struggled to catch up. Next there was a tight cluster of four ponies who were bumping and jostling each other as they ran. The rest of the racers were spread out behind, with a group of stragglers bringing up the rear.

"Look—Blossom's so far ahead of the pack!" said Pippa.

"No one can catch her now," Stardust whinnied. "I'm sure she'll win."

Excitement buzzed in Pippa's stomach. She couldn't wait to see Cinders's face when Blossom won the Equestriathon trophy. And what would Blossom's parents say? They might be show ponies, but Pippa felt sure they'd be thrilled and proud of their daughter.

"You can do it, Blossom!" Pippa called.

Stardust joined in, chanting, "Blossom, Blossom, Blossom!"

She trotted on the spot, bouncing Pippa up and down. It was so much fun that at first Pippa didn't notice that something was moving out at sea. Faster and faster, two shapes were swimming toward the shore, where they started dancing in the water. That got Pippa's attention. She put her hand up to shield her eyes from the sun.

"The seahorses are back," she gasped.

But what were they doing? Suddenly, Pippa realized that they must want to speak to her.

"Who are you waving at?" Stardust asked, as Pippa threw both arms in the air.

"Rosella and Triton," Pippa answered,

sliding from Stardust's back. "They're calling me."

"I'll take you down to the path to the beach," said Stardust.

Pippa hesitated. Riding Stardust would be much quicker than going by foot, but what about Blossom? They had promised to watch her race.

"Thanks, but you'd better stay here. If Blossom gallops past when we're on our way down the cliff path, she won't see you cheering her on and she'll be so disappointed."

"You're right," Stardust said with a big sigh. "Why does being a best friend have to be so difficult sometimes?"

"I don't know," said Pippa. She climbed down from Stardust's back and, stroking her softly on the nose, added, "But it's worth it."

"Definitely," Stardust agreed, nudging Pippa's hand.

"I won't be long. With any luck, I'll be back for the end of the race."

Pippa set off at a run, racing across the land as if she were in the Equestriathon herself. The ground was bumpy and covered in long, spiky grass that whipped against her legs. She gritted her teeth and ignored it. She ran so fast that she almost missed the path. Pulling up sharply, Pippa turned left and stumbled down the steep track. Stones rattled under her feet, and once she slipped and nearly fell. Throwing her arms out to save herself, she flushed hot with panic. Luckily, she regained her balance and kept going, more slowly this time.

Far away, the seahorses watched, bobbing up and down in the water so urgently that Pippa thought this must be an emergency. The path turned abruptly, catching Pippa totally unaware and causing her to trip. One minute she was running, the next she was pitching headfirst down the path. She was so shocked that her heart skipped a beat. Instinctively, she curled into a ball. She tumbled to the ground, hitting the path with a dull thud and rolling a short distance, until she stopped.

"Ouch!"

Now her heart was banging like

a crazy drum. Everything ached. Carefully, Pippa sat up and tested her arms and legs. She was amazed and relieved to discover that nothing was broken. Dusting the dirt and grit from her clothes, she took several deep breaths to steady herself, then stood up slowly.

Out at sea the seahorses seemed to be still now. Pippa waved to show that she wasn't hurt. But as she started off again, something pinged against her ankle. Stopping, she stared at her foot.

"Oh no!" Pippa said.

The strap of her sandal had snapped, leaving the shoe hanging uselessly off her foot. Pippa stared at it for a moment, then quickly tied the broken ends together. The strap wasn't long enough and kept coming undone. She pulled a crumpled tissue from her pocket and wound it around the broken strap like a bandage. But as soon as she took a step, the tissue fell away. Angrily, Pippa pulled the sandal off. Now what was she going to do?

Chapter 5

There was only one solution. Unbuckling the other sandal, Pippa slid it off, then, holding a shoe in each hand, she bravely set out again. Dust oozed between her toes and tiny stones bit into her feet. Pippa ran on, gasping with pain and hobbling each time she stepped on a really sharp stone. She was much slower without shoes, but she continued down the winding cliff path as fast as she could. She just hoped the seahorses would wait for her.

At last, the path flattened out and she could see the beach ahead. With an extra spurt of speed, Pippa ran onto the white sand, squealing with delight at the softness. Faster now, she hurtled across the beach and splashed into the sea. The water was deliciously cold and soothing to her aching feet. She waded out until the sea reached her knees.

The seahorses met her, their enormous curved tails brushing the ocean floor. Dipping their heads, they each touched their noses against Pippa's.

"Well done," Rosella said, her eyes sparkling proudly.

"You were very brave just now," added Triton, his voice gentle and deep.

Pippa flushed. She didn't feel brave—more annoyed that she'd fallen and broken her shoe.

"Have you found something?" she asked.

"I believe we have," said Triton.

Pippa's heart leaped with joy, then instantly sank as she could tell from the seahorses' nervous faces that it wasn't all good news.

"Is it a horseshoe?" she asked.

"We think so," said Rosella. "Something shiny and glittery is wedged in the rocks at the end of that jut of land. Can you see it?"

Pippa stared into the distance. She could see the rocks—three of them, with jagged tops and steep sides—but that was all. She took a step sideways and saw something flash.

"Yes," she said, her voice rising with excitement. "There's definitely something sparkly between the middle and end rocks."

"You'll have to hurry," warned Triton. "The tide has turned and very soon those rocks will be underwater."

"Once the sea comes in, it will be too late," added Rosella. "There's a nasty whirlpool around those rocks. It's very dangerous. Even with our magic we're not strong enough to get close to them."

Pippa looked at the rocks. They were so far away and the sea was rapidly creeping up them. Suddenly she felt very small and alone. Could she really do this by herself?

"I have to!" she said forcefully.

Pippa rushed along the beach. The sand was soft under her bare feet but running down the path from the cliffs had taken more out of her than she'd realized. The muscles in her legs ached with every step. She could feel herself slowing, and no matter how hard she tried, she couldn't make her legs work any faster. She knew the water was bubbling up the beach, its frothy white fingers curling around the rocks. What if the tide beat her and the whirlpool pulled the golden horseshoe loose, whisking it out to sea?

"No!" she panted. She couldn't let that happen. All eight of the golden horseshoes had to be in place on the Whispering Wall in time for Midsummer Day so that their magical energy could be renewed and Chevalia would be safe.

There was such a long way to go. It seemed hopeless, but Pippa didn't give up. On she ran, her heart pounding loudly in her ears, blocking out all other sounds. It was only when a shadow fell over her that she realized she wasn't alone.

"Stardust!" she squealed.

"You were gone such a long time I was starting to worry. I had to come and check you were okay. Get on my back," Stardust called, slowing to a walk.

"I'm so happy to see you!" exclaimed Pippa.

"Well, what are best friends for?"

Pippa stumbled alongside her. Her legs were trembling and she didn't think she had enough energy to jump onto Stardust's back. Stardust seemed to realize this because she stopped and knelt down on her front legs.

"I hope Mrs. Steeplechase isn't watching right now!" she joked.

Pippa couldn't help laughing too. The royal nanny was so strict she wouldn't care if all seven of the missing horseshoes were in danger of being swept out to sea—manners and behaving like a proper princess pony came first!

Climbing onto Stardust's back, Pippa sank her hands into her silky mane and wound it around them.

"Comfortable?"

"Very," said Pippa.

She lurched sideways as Stardust rose up, only just remembering to squeeze her legs into Stardust's sides to prevent herself from sliding over the pony's head.

"Let's go," Stardust called, bucking with excitement as she raced away.

Pippa leaned forward like a jockey, taking some of her weight from

Stardust's back as they galloped across the beach. Sand sprayed up from Stardust's hooves and her long white tail streamed behind her like a silky banner.

Was it her imagination or was the sea coming in even faster now? Pippa couldn't take her eyes off it as she willed it to slow down. It was no good. The sea closed in, licking against the bottom of the rocks and becoming deeper and deeper, until it spun around them in circles, like water whirling around a drain.

"Faster!" Pippa cried.

She threw herself flat against Stardust's neck. Stardust galloped harder, her breath coming in noisy rasps. Slowly, the rocks came closer, but poor Stardust was exhausted. As the pony lost speed, Pippa could hardly watch the sea's greedy blue fingers reaching up the rocks to the glittering object wedged there.

Bravely, Stardust galloped on but her stride was shorter and she kept

stumbling. Now that they were closer, there was no doubt that the glittering object was a golden horseshoe. But there was still some distance to go to reach it. A white wave lapped over the horseshoe.

"Oh no!" groaned Pippa.

They'd finally found the second horseshoe, but any second now they were about to lose it again.

Chapter 6

A pony was thundering up behind them, neighing loudly. Was it Mrs. Steeplechase? Pippa was afraid to look. But no, surely the royal nanny was too large to gallop that fast. Turning her head, she saw that it was Blossom.

"Blossom!" exclaimed Pippa. "What are you doing here?"

"When the racecourse turned a corner I saw you both from the cliff top.

You promised you'd watch me and I knew you wouldn't let me down, so I guessed something must be wrong if you were here on the beach. What's happened?"

"We've found one of the golden horseshoes," Pippa said, pointing at the distant rocks. "But it's almost underwater!"

"You won't get there in time to retrieve it," Blossom said, galloping beside Stardust. "I'll go for you."

Relief swept through Pippa but it was quickly replaced with despair.

"What about the race? You were in the lead."

"I pulled out. Chevalia matters far more than the race." Blossom snorted.

"Besides, winning isn't everything. Helping your friends is much more important."

"But how will you get the horseshoe off the rocks?"

"With my hooves," Blossom said bravely.

Pippa shook her head. The whirlpool was already too strong. Blossom would need all four hooves on the ground to stay safe.

"I'll come with you," she declared.

"There isn't time to stop for you," called Blossom, who was starting to pull ahead of Stardust.

If Blossom was making sacrifices and putting herself in danger, then Pippa must too.

"You don't have to stop. Come closer and I'll jump on your back," she shouted.

"Pippa, no!" shouted Stardust. "It's too dangerous. And you're scared of heights."

But Pippa was too busy concentrating to answer. As Blossom moved closer, Pippa noticed that Blossom was taller than Stardust. Could she manage to jump from one pony to the other without falling off? With a shudder, she ignored the pounding sound of Stardust's and Blossom's hooves.

Blossom matched her pace to Stardust's until she was exactly alongside her, then she closed the gap between them.

"Ready?" Blossom called.

Pippa swallowed hard. She felt dizzy suddenly but there was no time to lose. She reached out for Blossom's mane. It was still braided from the dressage competition so there wasn't much for her to hold on to. And how did she think she was going to get her legs over? Pippa realized that she would have to get into a crouching position to jump from Stardust's to Blossom's back. Pippa stared at the ground tearing by. It seemed like a very long way down.

I can't do it, said a scared little voice inside her head. But Pippa had already done so much on Chevalia that she'd never thought possible. Gathering all

her courage, she held on tightly to
Stardust's mane. She decided she would
do it on the count of three.

One, two, and . . . three.

Slowly, she leaned forward and
brought her feet up behind her, onto
Stardust's back. Seeing the ground
moving so fast beneath her made her

feel a little bit sick. Pippa refused to think about that. She fixed her gaze on Stardust's mane as she got her feet in the right position. Her heart was racing in time with Stardust's hoofbeats and her mouth was dry. Pippa took a long, deep breath. She pushed herself up so she was crouching on Stardust's back. Now all she had to do was to jump over to Blossom. Pippa reached out for Blossom's braided mane.

"I'm ready," she called.

"Be careful," shouted Stardust.

Pippa hesitated. Her head was spinning.

"Are you sure about this?" called Stardust.

Pippa didn't answer. She summoned

up every last bit of courage—and leaped!

Her stomach dipped. She seemed to hang in the air forever, but it was only a few seconds before she landed with a bump on the other pony's back. Blossom was wider than Stardust and had a much bouncier stride. Pippa was flung up and down for a moment, then, losing her balance, she slid sideways.

"Help!" she squeaked.

Pippa hung on, her legs gripping more tightly around Blossom's sides. Blossom misunderstood this move-ment—thinking that Pippa was asking her to go faster, she sped up. Lurching forward, Pippa desperately clung to Blossom's braids. She couldn't fall off now—there wasn't time! She pulled herself to the middle of Blossom's back. She knew that she had been very lucky that nothing had gone wrong so far. Now that she had regained her balance, Pippa leaned forward and urged Blossom on.

"Go, Blossom! Go, Pippa!" Stardust called, as Blossom galloped ahead.

Only the tops of the rocks were visible now. Blossom raced across the glistening, wet beach and into the sea, her steps slowing as the water deepened.

"Careful," Pippa said, feeling Blossom strain against the current.

"Look!" cried Blossom. "The horse-shoe!"

It was upside down, wedged between two rocks.

Just then a large wave crashed into Blossom, making her stumble.

"Eeek!" Pippa shrieked, as the wave soaked her too.

"Sorry," said Blossom.

The ocean floor was uneven and covered in slippery seaweed. Pippa was amazed at how steady Blossom was as she waded on.

"Don't ever let anyone tell you that you're clumsy," Pippa told her.

"I'm not now, am I?" Blossom said happily. "It's because I'm really concentrating and I'm not worrying that everyone is watching and laughing at me."

When they were just an arm's length away from the rocks, Blossom suddenly stopped and wavered.

"Oh, horseflies!" she exclaimed. "The current's too strong. This is as close as I can get!"

Chapter 7

Pippa stared at the rocks. Beneath her, the water swirled and bubbled like a giant's cooking pot. If she fell off Blossom trying to reach the horseshoe, she'd never be able to swim against the current.

I'm not going to fall, she told herself. But Blossom's legs were buckling against the force of the whirlpool.

"Blossom, can you stand very still while I climb up your neck?"

"Yes," said Blossom, "but hurry! The tide's coming in really fast, and I can feel the whirlpool sucking at my legs."

Pippa quickly pulled herself toward Blossom's head. She clutched Blossom's mane with one hand and leaned over to the rocks. If only she could stretch a little bit farther . . . Growing red in the face, Pippa reached out until her fingers were brushing the horseshoe. It was almost in her grasp.

Almost.

But the horseshoe was wedged firmly between the rocks and just couldn't be pulled free.

"Please hurry," Blossom said urgently.

It was no good. The task needed two hands. Pippa let go of Blossom's mane

and tried again. The horseshoe budged by the tiniest amount, then stuck tight. Carefully, Pippa wriggled it backward and forward. It reminded her of wobbling a loose tooth. She rocked the horseshoe forward and backward until it shifted a bit more.

"Hurry!" whinnied Blossom.

The water was still rising and was splashing around Pippa's bare feet now. She yanked the horseshoe as hard as she could.

Over the roar of the whirlpool, Pippa thought she could hear Stardust calling her name from the shore. It made her feel braver to know that her best friend was cheering her on.

With all her might, she pulled at the horseshoe again. She felt it scrape against the rock, then suddenly the golden horseshoe came free. The suddenness took her by surprise, and she slid backward, almost losing her balance. Wildly, Pippa grabbed Blossom's mane. As she did so, the horseshoe slipped through her fingers.

"No!" Pippa snatched at it, trapping it against Blossom's neck and only just preventing it from dropping into the churning water.

"I caught it!" she yelled.

Immediately Blossom swung around to face the beach, and then froze in her tracks. Standing in the water a few hooves away were two scruffy ponies.

"Night Mares!" Pippa gasped, recognizing Eclipse and Nightshade from the previous day and realizing that they were the ponies she had seen at the edge of the Wild Forest.

"Give that back," Eclipse said in a mean voice.

"It belongs to us," said Nightshade.

The water was rising even higher

now, and Pippa worried that they'd all be carried out to sea.

"PIPPA!" Stardust called from the shore.

Stardust's cry gave Pippa an idea.

"This horseshoe belongs on the Whispering Wall," said Pippa. Then she shouted to Stardust, "Catch!"

Pippa hurled the horseshoe into the air and Stardust galloped to catch it in her mouth.

"NO!" cried Eclipse.

"Let's get out of here," Pippa said to Blossom.

Blossom waded back toward the beach, and Pippa turned to see Nightshade and Eclipse still standing in the water, staring up at the cliffs. Pippa followed their gaze and saw the mysterious cloaked pony looking down at them. The two Night Mares were just standing, as if glued to the spot, in the rising water.

"You two!" Pippa called, as Blossom pushed farther toward the shore. "Get out of the water—it's dangerous!"

Pippa felt Blossom's muscles tighten as she bravely fought against the tide. One careful hoof at a time, she waded back to the beach. Clutching Blossom's mane tightly, Pippa cheered her on until, at last, they were back on dry sand.

"That was close," said Blossom.

"Too close," agreed Pippa.

Stardust trotted up to Blossom and Pippa and gave the horseshoe to Pippa to hold.

"I tried to call to you," she said. "Those Night Mares came out of nowhere."

"They were watching us," said Pippa. "And there was someone else watching too."

"Who?" asked Stardust.

Pippa pointed to the top of the cliff, but the cloaked pony had vanished. She then turned to check on the Night Mares in the water—they were soggy and defeated, but wading clumsily through the shallows.

"I don't know," admitted Pippa. "But I do know that we should get this horseshoe back where it belongs—on the Whispering Wall!"

Stardust darted next to Blossom and, side by side, they raced across the beach, leaving the Night Mares behind.

Pippa looked back to see the Night Mares emerge from the water. They started to come after Pippa and her friends, but the gap was too big for them to catch up. With an angry toss of their heads, they turned and galloped away in the opposite direction.

Blossom and Stardust began to climb the steep cliff path.

"You did it!" Stardust said, her dark eyes shining with happiness.

"We all did it," said Pippa. "Together!"

"I'm glad I have two best friends," said Stardust.

"Look," Blossom cried suddenly. "The giant seahorses are watching."

Pippa proudly waved the golden horseshoe above her head. The seahorses reared up in delight. Droplets of water flew from their spiky manes, falling

like silvery fountains. Pippa sighed happily as she prepared to slide from Blossom's back.

"Don't get down yet," said Blossom. "I don't feel tired now."

"What about the race?" Pippa asked. "Don't you want to go back and finish it and get a medal?"

Blossom shook her head. "There's always next year. I'll definitely enter the Equestriathon again, but right now I've got something that's much more important than a medal—two best friends."

"Best friends forever!" said Stardust.

"Forever," Pippa and Blossom agreed.

Slowly, they went back up the path, stopping to pick up Pippa's sandals.

"Oh, I don't even remember dropping them," said Pippa. "I'll have to go barefoot. They're broken."

"Don't worry, the royal blacksmith will fix them for you," said Stardust.

Excitedly, they made their way back to the Royal Games grounds on the Fields. It was impossible to keep the horseshoe a secret. When they approached the show arena, a crowd of ponies quickly gathered to greet and cheer for them. Pippa blushed deep red as some of the bolder ponies reached out to touch her with their noses as she passed.

The queen and king were in the royal box watching the end of the Equestria-thon. Pippa slid from Blossom's back as Stardust led the way in. Quick as a flash, Cinders came out of her own box to block Blossom from following them.

"Only members of the Royal Court are allowed in here," she said nastily.

But the queen had already seen that

Pippa was carrying a horseshoe and she excitedly waved Blossom in.

"It's not fair," Cinders hissed to her mother, Baroness Divine.

The baroness narrowed her eyes. "Good things come to those who wait," she whispered back.

Pippa wondered why Baroness Divine never had anything nice to say, especially now, when they'd found another of the missing horseshoes. She soon forgot the baroness, though, as she dropped a curtsy to Queen Moonshine. The queen was the most beautiful pony she'd ever seen. Her golden coat seemed to glow and her pure white tail fell elegantly to the ground.

The queen's face lit up with joy.

"The second missing horseshoe," she whinnied. "That's wonderful news. I'm very proud of you all."

King Firestar stamped his hoof in agreement. "We must put the horseshoe right back where it belongs," he said seriously.

A look of worry crossed the queen's face. "But it's almost time to award the prizes."

"Stardust and her friends have proved themselves trustworthy and reliable. They could take the horseshoe back," King Firestar suggested.

"Yes, please do," the queen replied.

Pippa was secretly pleased. There was something special about the golden horseshoe. Holding it gave her a tingling feeling that made her think the magic was rubbing off on her somehow. It gave her courage.

When they reached Stableside Castle's courtyard, Pippa stood up on Blossom's back and carefully hung the

horseshoe on the ancient stone wall. The three friends stood back to admire it as it sparkled prettily in the late-afternoon sun.

"Two horseshoes are safe." Stardust sighed, staring up at them in wonder.

"Our quest isn't over yet," said Pippa. "There are still six to find."

"You've done enough for one day, child," the king said, striding into the Royal Courtyard. He was accompanied by two ponies, with gleaming chestnut coats, who Pippa didn't recognize.

"Mom and Dad!" said Blossom.

"I thought you were staying to award the prizes," Stardust said to her dad.

"When a father is proud of his daughter," said the king, "he should tell her."

"And that goes for show ponies too," boomed Blossom's dad. "You made your mom and me very proud today. We never realized how fast you were. If you want to keep racing instead of doing dressage, you have our full support."

Blossom beamed with delight. "Thank you," she whinnied.

"Now let's go back to the Games grounds," said the king. "You three deserve to have some fun—and we've got the evening's entertainment ahead."

"A banquet, dancing, and a huge fireworks display at the end," Stardust said happily.

"Oh, I love fireworks!" said Pippa.

☆

Long troughs had been put up in the main arena of the Royal Games grounds, and serving ponies were filling them with crunchy caramel apples, sugar-toasted oats, and candied carrots. Music was playing, colored disco lights were flashing, and lots of ponies were dancing together.

The three best friends ducked under the horseshoe arch, but as they started for the arena Pippa heard someone shout, "They're back!"

At once the music stopped and the disco lights went out. The dancers became still and the crowd fell silent. Pippa flushed as all eyes turned toward her, Stardust, and Blossom. The queen was in the royal box and she waved them forward.

"Your determination and courage have resulted in another horseshoe hanging back where it belongs," Queen Moonshine said in a clear voice. "The Royal Ponies and the ponies of Chevalia thank you. Blossom, you have shown yourself to be a true friend of Chevalia. By putting the island's needs before your own, you missed out on winning a prize in the Equestriathon. For your courage and true selflessness, you deserve a special award. Step forward."

Nervously, Blossom did so. The queen smiled as she placed a glittering tiara on her head. The sparkling gemstones were designed as a blue rosette, like a flower in bloom.

"To Chevalia," said the queen.

"To Chevalia," cheered everyone, with Pippa, Stardust, and Blossom cheering the loudest.

Princess Ponies

Ponies

The Special Secret

Chapter 1

"Look how blue the sky is this morning," said Pippa MacDonald. She was admiring the pretty view of the island from a window high up in Stableside Castle.

"It's always lovely here on Chevalia," Princess Stardust said, carefully braiding red ribbons into her long white mane.

It might not be if you don't hurry up, Pippa thought.

It wasn't Stardust's fault that as a princess pony, and seventh in line to the throne, she was expected to always look her best. And it certainly wasn't Stardust's fault that the island of Chevalia was in danger.

Pippa picked up a comb and started brushing Stardust's tail. It was so long it hung down to the floor and Pippa had to kneel to reach it. She could still hardly believe that, while on vacation with her family, she'd been brought to Chevalia, a magical island where ponies can talk. Pippa had discovered that Chevalia was in grave danger. The eight golden horseshoes that gave life to the island had been stolen from the ancient wall in the castle courtyard. If they weren't all back in their places on Midsummer Day, so that they could have their magical energy renewed by the Midsummer sun, then Chevalia would fade away.

With Stardust's help Pippa had already found two horseshoes, but now there were just four days until Midsummer, and six horseshoes were still missing.

Placing the comb on the dresser, Pippa stood back to admire her work. Then she put on the pretty dress that had magically appeared overnight and was neatly laid out for her on a chair.

"Can we search the Horseshoe Hills today?" she asked.

"But it's Harvest Day," Stardust said, studying her reflection in a long mirror.

"Everyone who attends Canter's Prep School for Fine Equine is expected to go to the Grasslands to bring the harvest home. That includes me."

"Oh!" Pippa's heart sank.

Even though Chevalia was under threat, Stardust's parents, Queen Moonshine and King Firestar, were determined that the Royal Family continue their many traditions so as not to worry everyone.

"Harvest Day is fun," Stardust assured her. "And it's not all work. The best part is the picnic lunch—it's like a party with all our favorite things to eat, like carrots dipped in linseed oil."

"I suppose we haven't searched the Grasslands yet," said Pippa.

"Then we'll do it today while we're helping with the harvest," Stardust said decisively.

Pippa wasn't sure how much searching they would have time for if they were expected to work, but it was better than nothing.

"Let's go then," she said, eager to get started.

After a quick breakfast in the castle's huge dining room, Pippa, Stardust, and the four of her brothers and sisters who still attended Canter's Prep School followed their nanny, Mrs. Steeplechase, down to the Grasslands.

"Stop it," Pippa whispered, trying

9

not to giggle as Stardust imitated the way her teacher waddled.

"No talking!" Mrs. Steeplechase said, turning around to glare at them.

"Sorry," said Pippa. She turned her attention to the lines of ponies who were approaching the Grasslands from every direction. There were lots of

foals, their manes and tails braided with purple ribbons, trotting beside their parents.

"They're from Canter's Nursery School," Stardust explained. "The babies wear purple ribbons, the toddlers wear red ribbons like me, and the older kids wear blue ones. We should have braided ribbons in your hair too. When we get to the Grasslands, I'll ask if anyone has any extra ribbon so you're not left out."

"Thanks," Pippa said absently, her mind on the missing horseshoes. She really hoped that they would find at least one today.

The Grasslands were going to be difficult to search. The grass grew so tall that in places it was higher than Pippa's head. It was like walking through a pale-green forest. Soon they came out of the grass and into a clearing. To Pippa's surprise there was a small farmhouse with a large yard.

"Mucker!" squealed Stardust. Breaking away from the group, she trotted over to a stocky dark-brown pony with a white blaze, four white stockings, and a black mane and tail.

"Princess Stardust!"

Stardust and Mucker brushed noses.

"I'm so glad you've come to help with the harvest. I've heard lots about you," he added, shyly nodding at Pippa. "You're here to save Chevalia."

Pippa blushed as red as a strawberry.

Everyone had such high hopes for her. She didn't want to let Chevalia down.

Stardust's big sister, Princess Crystal, was standing in the middle of the farm-yard putting ponies into groups. As first in line to the throne of Chevalia, she was expected to help supervise the younger ponies on Harvest Day.

"No talking!" Crystal yelled as she looked at her clipboard. "Stardust and Pippa, you're with—eeek!"

Crystal let out a huge shriek and, dropping her clipboard, galloped full speed across the yard.

Stardust snorted with laughter, then quickly turned it into a cough as Crystal trotted back, her nose in the air as if nothing had happened.

"It was a horsefly," Stardust explained to a puzzled Pippa. "Crystal's terrified of them."

Crystal nervously batted the air with her clipboard in case the horsefly returned. She continued, "Stardust and Pippa are with Mucker."

Mucker's face lit up. "Come on—I'll

show you both where to go," he said
happily.

Mucker led them out of the yard to
a muddy field full of tall grass with
stems as thick as bamboo shoots. A
group of ponies wearing red ribbons
were already hard at work. Their legs

and faces were splattered with mud and their coats were steaming. As Pippa and Stardust trotted over to the group with Mucker, he explained that it was very hard work harvesting the grass.

"It's much thicker than usual," said Mucker. "Dad can't understand it. He didn't do anything different this year."

The members of Mucker's family were farm ponies, and he loved working with them on the land. He gave Pippa some tools and showed her how to harvest the grass.

Pippa learned quickly and realized that she was beginning to enjoy the work. The grass may have been thick and strong but it made a soft, whispery noise as it was cut.

The whispering grew more insistent. Suddenly, Pippa realized it was a voice.

"What did you say?" she asked Stardust.

"Nothing," replied Stardust, who had a smudge of brown mud on her face.

Pippa was puzzled—she was sure

Stardust had said something. She continued cutting and after a while she heard Stardust speak again.

"Sorry, I didn't quite catch that," Pippa said.

"Catch what?" asked Stardust.

"What you just said."

Stardust looked strangely at Pippa. "I never said a word."

"But I can hear a voice. Listen!" Pippa added. "There it is again."

Stardust stood still, her ears twitching as she concentrated on listening. "Sorry," she said at last. "All I can hear is the buzz of horseflies, nothing else."

Pippa couldn't understand it. The buzzing voice was beginning to irritate her. Why couldn't Stardust hear it too?

"Well, look who it is," a voice said loudly—a different voice, but one that Pippa knew. "It's Princess Grunge and her best friend, Dirt Girl!"

Pippa turned around and faced Cinders, the meanest pony in the Royal Court.

Chapter 2

"So now we know," Cinders said loudly, her eyes narrowing.

"Know what?" asked Stardust.

"That you're a fake." Cinders gave a high-pitched laugh. "You can't be a princess because a real princess would never get her hooves dirty. You're just an ordinary farm pony like Mucker."

"Of course I'm a real princess," Stardust said angrily.

"No, you're not," Cinders replied. "That's what my mom says anyway."

With that, Cinders swept past Stardust, taking great care not to step in the mud.

Stardust's brown eyes glittered with tears. "What did she mean?" she asked.

"Ignore her," Pippa said, stroking

Stardust's mud-splattered nose. "She was just being nasty to upset you."

"Are you sure?"

"Yes," Pippa said, even though she wasn't convinced. Cinders had sounded threatening and as if she knew something, but Pippa didn't want to frighten Stardust. She continued to stroke her nose, until she stopped shaking and calmed down.

"Cinders is right, though," Stardust said at last. "If I have to help with the harvest, then I should be given a cleaner job."

Mucker let out a snort of surprise. "Getting dirty has never bothered you before. We've always had a lot of fun together on the farm."

"Not anymore," Stardust said firmly. "It's time I started acting like a real princess."

To Mucker's dismay, Stardust flatly refused to help further. Instead she tore up some grass and used it to wipe the mud from her face, legs, and hooves.

"I'm going to ask Crystal for something else to do," she announced. "Something cleaner and more worthy of a princess pony." And she trotted off.

"I'll never get to see Stardust if she stops visiting the farm," Mucker said sadly. "I'd love to visit her at the castle but that's not going to happen—not when I come from a farming family. Besides, I'm too busy with farmwork to attend the Royal Court."

Pippa started to go after Stardust but quickly changed her mind. Poor Mucker was so upset—she couldn't leave him now. Keeping one eye on Stardust, she continued to help with the harvest while also keeping a lookout for shiny objects in the mud.

It was a long, hard morning. Pippa's back ached and her hands grew sore from gripping her tools and from all the cutting work. In the distance she could see that Stardust wasn't making much progress with her new job of collecting the cut grass. A cloud of horseflies was buzzing around her head, and each time Stardust swatted them away with her tail they just flew at her again.

"Go away, you awful things," Stardust shouted, angrily stomping a hoof.

The horseflies were becoming even more agitated. Buzzing loudly, they flew in circles around Stardust's head. Pippa ran over to see if she could help. But after swatting repeatedly at the horse-flies with her hands, she realized that it wasn't making any difference. She stood still and listened. The horseflies were making the same funny buzzing noise, like whispery voices, that she'd heard earlier. She decided to try something.

"Anyone would think that the horseflies were trying to talk to you," Pippa said.

Stardust stopped being cross and whinnied with laughter. "Talking horseflies? That's crazy!" she exclaimed. "That's the funniest thing I've heard all morning. Oh, look—there's Mucker's older brother, Trojan. He helps run the farm with Mucker's dad. He must have come to check on us. Let's say hello."

"Wait," Pippa said, still trying to figure out if she was imagining things or if the horseflies really were trying to tell them something.

But Stardust was already on her way over to the two brothers. Pippa followed.

"Hi, Trojan. Have you come to help or are you here to boss us around like Crystal?" she asked.

Trojan blushed at the mention of Crystal.

"Mucker and I were just discussing the best way to harvest the grass," he said gruffly. "But if Crystal's here I'm sure everything is under control."

Trojan's dark-brown coat still looked ruddy as he hurried away.

"Did I say the wrong thing?" asked Stardust.

"Well, Trojan really likes Crystal, but she barely notices him," Mucker explained. "Don't say I told you that, though!"

Stardust giggled. "Poor Trojan, liking my bossy big sister!"

"I think we should get back to work," Mucker said.

"He's right," Pippa said. "The Grasslands are so much bigger than I expected. We're never going to get all the harvest in *and* look for horseshoes in one day."

"It doesn't matter if the harvesting isn't finished today, but we do have to find the horseshoes quickly," Stardust said thoughtfully. "Let's go down to the stream—we haven't searched that area yet. The grass is much shorter near the stream, and we can have our picnic lunch there too."

"But I haven't finished looking here," said Pippa.

"We can come back later," Stardust replied.

"We should finish searching this area first," Pippa said firmly. "We should search each area properly before we move on to the next one; otherwise we might miss something."

A mixture of emotions flashed across Stardust's face, but at last she said, "You're right, Pippa. I'm so glad you're here to help—I'm definitely not as organized as you are. Let's search this part of the Grasslands thoroughly before lunch."

Pippa and Stardust slowly moved away from their harvesting group and put their efforts into searching for the horseshoes.

"We shouldn't make it too obvious that we've stopped harvesting," Stardust said quietly. "Remember that Mom and Dad want us to carry on as normal so we don't frighten anyone."

Every now and then Pippa heard Cinders's voice across the field. She was even bossier than Crystal, ordering the younger ponies around and avoiding getting her own hooves dirty.

"Anyone would think *her* mom was the queen and not jusssst a baronesssss," a tiny voice buzzed in her ear.

Pippa jumped with surprise. "Who's

that?" she asked, searching around the field.

"Mmmmeeee," hummed the voice.

Thinking she must be imagining things, Pippa tapped her ear with her hand.

"Careful! You nearly sssswatted meee."

A large horsefly darted in front of Pippa and hovered by her nose. She blinked in amazement.

"You!" she exclaimed. "Was that you talking to me?"

"Yesssss. My name is Zimb. Weeee've been trying to talk to Princess Stardust all morning but she just won't lissssssten," he said, waving his three friends over.

"We neeeeed help," the horseflies

said. "Pleasssse say that you'll help ussss or we're all going to be in great danger."

Chapter 3

"Two ponies came to see us out here on the Grasslands," explained Zimb, the largest of the horseflies. "They told us the Mistresssss had sent them on behalf of every pony in Chevalia because she wants to make peace with us and to be friendsss forever. They gave us two golden horseshoesss to prove they meant what they said. We were ssso excited. We've been trying to make

friendsssss with the ponies for ages. But
then we learned that the golden horseshoesss had been stolen and that this
put Chevalia in serious danger. The
Mistressssss tricked us."

The Mistress! Pippa had no idea who
she was, but each time they came close
to finding a horseshoe her name came
up. Pippa wondered whether this mysterious Mistress was behind the disap-
pearance of all the horseshoes.

"Who is this Mistress?" she asked.

"You know, the hooded pony with the
big cloak," the horseflies said excitedly.

As Pippa was taking this in, the
horseflies continued, "We wanted to
return the horseshoesss to the king and
queen but we can't find the place where

we left them. The grassss has grown too long. Can you help ussss?"

Something clicked in Pippa's head.

"That's it!" she cried. "So there are definitely two horseshoes here in the Grasslands."

She quickly ran to Stardust and filled her in on what the horseflies had told her, adding, "That's why the grass has grown so long—it's because of the magic from the two horseshoes."

Stardust was amazed but she was even more surprised that Pippa had heard the horseflies talking.

"I had no idea that horseflies could speak!" she whinnied. "But then I've never really listened to their buzzing."

As Stardust and Pippa set about

finding the two horseshoes, they grew hungry and even more tired. When they stopped for a short break, Pippa had a thought.

"If the magic from the horseshoes has made the grass grow taller than normal, then they must be buried where the grass is longest."

"Of course!" exclaimed Stardust. She nuzzled Pippa's arm. "You're so clever."

"You're clever too," Pippa said modestly.

Stardust turned pink with delight. Puffing out her chest, she said, "Let's go and ask Mucker where the longest grass is. He knows these fields like the back of his hoof!"

"Good idea," said Pippa.

They found Mucker with a group of ponies close to the stream and asked him where the longest grass was.

"Over there," Mucker said, pointing toward the water. "It's very muddy, though."

"I don't mind," said Pippa. She ran over to the stream and along the bank until she found an enormous clump of grass stretching high above her head. The ground was boggy and squishy. Pippa was glad her dress didn't have long sleeves as she sank her hands into the mud.

"Ew!" Stardust said, turning up her nose. "Careful, Pippa—you're getting mud everywhere!"

Pippa was too busy scooping up

handfuls of mud to hear Stardust. It was only when a deep voice boomed out, "What are you doing?" that she stopped digging.

"King Firestar." Pippa's face felt hot as she dropped him a curtsy. "We think two of the missing horseshoes might be buried here."

"Hmmm." The king looked at Stardust and he stared at her for a long time. "Let me tell you a story," he said at last. "I was a farm pony once. My family— your grandparents, Stardust—owned a huge farm and everyone had to help out. I remember one Harvest Day in particular, when it had rained for weeks and the fields were even muddier than these are now." King Firestar poked the ground with his hoof and watched as black mud oozed over it. "Harvesting in the mud was fun, but there was one little pony who didn't think so. She was a pretty palomino princess. At first she was very prim and proper, standing with her hooves neatly together and refusing to help. But after a while she saw how much fun everyone was having. Fed up with being left out, she joined in the harvesting, and to her surprise she loved it. Her beautiful coat was covered in mud by the time the harvest was done but the princess didn't care. She just jumped in the stream to clean herself off. I fell in love with that princess pony and I've loved her ever since."

"Stop it! You're embarrassing me," said another familiar voice. "Besides, you tell that story every year."

"Your Majesty," Pippa said, curtsying.

"How is the harvest coming along?" the queen asked, her magnificent palomino coat gleaming in the sunlight. "Is everyone working hard?"

Mucker stepped forward. "Yes, Your Majesty," he said, too loyal to give Stardust away.

Stardust hung her head in shame. "I think I could work harder," she mumbled.

"Don't let us stop you then," said the queen. "There's enough time to do a bit more before lunch."

As the queen and king moved away, Stardust began to dig in the mud. Soon she was muddy up to her knees, but her dirt-stained face glowed with happiness.

"Dad was right. This is really fun," she said, kicking up more mud. "Look at Crystal and Trojan over there. Wouldn't it be fun if they followed in Mom and Dad's hoofsteps and got married?"

"Ssssh!" Pippa giggled. "You're not supposed to say anything about that."

"Who's getting married?" Crystal called, trotting over. "And what are you doing digging around in the mud, Stardust?"

Stardust tried not to giggle. "We're looking for missing horseshoes," she replied, and then quickly told her what the horseflies had said.

"Well, don't let me hold you up," Crystal said, walking off to check on another group of ponies who were working nearby.

☆

Just before they stopped for lunch, there was a light rain shower, which made the ground even muddier.

"Look at Cinders," Pippa said, as she watched the pony take cover in the barn.

"She's done even less work than me," said Stardust.

"But she's having less fun than you," commented Pippa, who loved the feel of the mud and didn't care how dirty she got. "Ouch! What was that?"

Her heart skipped a beat as her fingers touched something cold. Pippa frantically scooped away the mud under her. It was up to her elbows but she hardly noticed it. She was on to something! She could feel the magic tingling in her fingers as they scraped away at the object buried in the sticky ground.

"I'm almost there," Pippa panted, while Stardust watched anxiously.

Wrapping her fingers around her find, Pippa pulled. But the object was stuck.

"Let me help," Stardust said, gently taking the hem of Pippa's dress in her mouth so that she could pull her backward.

"One, two, three, *pull!*" yelled Pippa.

There was a loud noise, like water being sucked down a drain, then she and Stardust fell back as the object was suddenly worked free. They landed in an enormous patch of mud.

"Yes!" Pippa shouted, holding up the object in delight. "It's a very dirty golden horseshoe!"

"Hooray!" Stardust cheered, scrambling up onto her legs. "That's three horseshoes we've found now. And there's another one here somewhere. . . ."

Just then a gong sounded.

"Lunchtime," Stardust said. "Let's eat before we look for the fourth one."

"We should hang this horseshoe on the Whispering Wall first," Pippa said, even though she was famished.

"Let's eat first," said Stardust.

"But—" Pippa started to argue.

"We need to keep our strength up," Stardust said firmly. "Besides, taking one horseshoe back to the castle will waste too much time. Let's wait until we've found both of them."

"Okay," Pippa said reluctantly, but she knew that Stardust had a point.

She rinsed the horseshoe in the stream and cleaned away the dirt until it glittered. Then they made their way over to the huge portable troughs that were set out for lunch.

"When we find the other horse-shoe, we'll have found half of them," Pippa said.

"Oh!" Stardust exclaimed, her eyes shining with hope. "Then let's hurry up and eat lunch so we can find it!"

Chapter 4

The picnic was noisy and fun. Canter's ponies and all the farming ponies were covered in mud, their coats were matted, and their school ribbons were soaked and unraveling—but they were all relishing Harvest Day.

Only Cinders still looked neat—her chestnut coat shone, and her braided mane and tail were still held neatly in place with shiny red ribbons.

"Look at the state of you all," she said, wrinkling her nose.

No one was listening, though. They were too busy telling stories about their morning and admiring the golden horseshoe that Stardust and Pippa had propped on a tree at the picnic site. Pippa was still a little worried that they hadn't taken the horseshoe back to the castle, and she mentioned her concerns to Stardust.

"Don't worry, the horseshoe will be fine," the princess pony said. "There are plenty of ponies around to look after it, and it would have been a shame to miss the picnic lunch."

Pippa had to agree. The castle's serving ponies had sent her a special packed

lunch that included a peanut butter and jelly sandwich, carrot sticks, strawberries, and a whole jug of fizzy peach juice. Everything looked delicious and it would be a pity to waste it.

"Okay, but when we go back to work, we should ask a pony to guard the horseshoe for us."

"Good idea," Stardust said, lowering her head into a trough of honeyed oats.

They were just finishing lunch when a swarm of horseflies flew at Stardust. The ponies next to her whinnied in alarm and Mucker trotted over, his head down.

"Get out of here, you pesky beasts," he snorted.

"Wait!" buzzed the horseflies. "We want to talk to the princess."

Mucker was about to charge at them but Stardust shouted, "Mucker, stop! Don't hurt them. They're my friends."

"Thank you, princess," Zimb said.

"You can talk to the horseflies?" Mucker's eyes nearly popped out of his head.

"It's easy. Pippa showed me how," said Stardust. "All you have to do is listen very carefully."

By now the rest of Canter's had stopped eating and were listening too. The nursery school foals were so in awe that they couldn't stop looking at Stardust. The only pony not impressed was Cinders.

"If you think I'm going to listen to a horsefly, think again," she snorted. "They're nothing but nasty pests. Ouch!" Cinders let out a neigh and started dancing around in irritation.

"Ssssorry," buzzed Zimb. "I didn't mean to bite you on the bottom. I tripped by accident. Honestly, I did!"

He sounded so insincere that Stardust burst out laughing. Cinders scowled and marched away angrily. Pippa bit her lip to stop herself from giggling. Even though Cinders was so unpleasant, she still felt a little bit sorry for her.

"We sssssaw that you found one of the horseshoesssss," buzzed Zimb.

"Yes," Stardust said. "And how did you do?"

"We found nothing," Zimb said sadly, "but we'll keep looking now we know how important it is to have all eight horseshoes back on the ancient wall in time for Midsummer Day. We're just sssssssorry that by accepting two of them from the Mistress we caused ssssso much trouble."

"It's not your fault. And thanks for all your help," Stardust said gratefully.

Pippa was deep in thought. Who was the Mistress? The question still bothered her. She looked up and noticed Cinders, who was lying on the ground by herself looking very sad and lonely. Pippa couldn't help but feel sorry for her, and she wandered over to her.

"Please, will you look after this horseshoe for us while we search for the other one?" Pippa asked.

Cinders looked very surprised, but she agreed. "All right," she said.

"Why did you ask her that?" Stardust whispered angrily when Pippa rejoined her. "She doesn't deserve such a special job. She's done nothing all morning."

Pippa shrugged. "Mom says you should always give people a chance to be nice. If we're kind to Cinders, then maybe she'll start being kind back."

Stardust nuzzled Pippa's arm with her nose. "Your mom sounds nice," she said.

"She is," Pippa said, feeling a little homesick. But at least Mom and her brother and sister wouldn't be missing her—Chevalia existed in a special time bubble so that Pippa could stay there for as long as she needed, while time stood still in her own world. She pushed the sad feeling away. "Let's get started," she said.

Pippa and Stardust searched and searched, until their fingers and hooves were sore from digging through the mud and dirt and grass.

It was late afternoon when Pippa said wearily, "Let's stop for a drink."

"Good idea." Stardust straightened up. She started to walk back to the stream, where there was a drinking trough with fresh running water, but she slipped on a patch of mud.

"Careful!" said Pippa.

"Ouch!" Stardust whinnied. "I stubbed my hoof on something hard."

Her eyes met Pippa's and they stared at each other for a split second. Then, wordlessly, they threw themselves to the ground and began scraping the mud away. Pippa's fingers touched something hard and cold. Her heart thudded with excitement. Could it be the other horseshoe that was missing in the Grasslands?

"We've found the fourth missing horseshoe!" squealed Stardust.

"Isn't it funny how sometimes you just stumble across the exact thing that you're trying so hard to find!" said Pippa, delighted. "How lucky!"

"Mom and Dad are going to be thrilled," said Stardust. "Two horse-shoes in one day! Come on, let's go and get the other one and take them both back to the castle."

Stardust scooped up the horseshoe in her mouth and they returned to the stream. Pippa was so happy, she felt like she was walking on air. But as they drew nearer, they saw that Cinders was hunched up and crying. A cold feeling came over Pippa as she hurried toward her.

"Cinders, what's wrong?" she asked.

"I . . . I . . . I'm sorry," said Cinders. "It wasn't my fault. I only left it for a minute.

A foal came and told me that you needed me urgently, but I couldn't find you and when I came back the horseshoe was gone."

"What?" shrieked Stardust. "You left the horseshoe unguarded? How could you be so careless?"

Pippa was so shocked, it was as if all the breath had been squeezed out of her. But she knew that getting upset with Cinders wasn't going to help.

"We all make mistakes," she said kindly. "How long ago did it happen?"

A strange look crossed Cinders's face, and for a fleeting moment Pippa thought she almost smiled, but then Cinders's brown eyes seemed so full of remorse.

"Not long," Cinders answered.

Pippa realized that they had to be smart if they were to have any hope of recovering the horseshoe.

"Right, let's organize a search party," she decided.

She looked around to see who was available. Prince Storm, Prince Comet,

Trojan, and Mucker had come over to see what all the noise was about. But there was no time to organize them into proper groups, because Pippa saw something else.

At the far end of the field were two scruffy ponies who were behaving very strangely. They were sneaking away on hoof tips from the Grasslands. Pippa recognized them instantly.

"Night Mares," she said, pointing. "Although they're not Nightshade and Eclipse this time." Seeing something shiny, she added, "And they've stolen our horseshoe."

Stardust gave the fourth golden horseshoe to Mucker to keep safe.

"Quick," she shouted. "After them!"

Chapter 5

"Jump on!" Stardust turned around to stand by Pippa.

Grabbing a handful of mane, Pippa jumped onto Stardust's back. She was barely astride her when Stardust took off at a fast gallop. They were almost across the field when the Night Mares realized they'd been seen, and they took off with a whinny of surprise.

Storm and Comet had already

galloped off toward the Savannah, hoping to catch the Night Mares as they made their way back to the Volcano.

"Hurry," Pippa urged, leaning forward like a jockey on a racing pony.

The mud was slowing Stardust down. Pippa could hear it squishing under her hooves, and some of it flicked up, splattering her own hands and face. Stardust struggled on, not caring about the mud, and slowly they began to catch up with the Night Mares.

"Go, Stardust!" Pippa yelled encouragingly.

"Hang on," Stardust shouted back. "I'm going to take a shortcut."

She changed direction, veering to the left and heading for a track. Pippa clutched Stardust's mane and gripped her flanks hard with her knees. She knew she had to concentrate on her balance. They couldn't risk losing sight of the Night Mares.

Pippa felt sick with excitement. If Stardust could keep this speed up, they would be able to cut the Night Mares off. She hunched low over Stardust's neck, her wavy brown hair flowing behind her.

Away to her left Pippa could hear a rattling noise. At first she ignored it, but the noise was growing steadily louder and was making Pippa uneasy. What was it? She looked around and gasped in horror. A cart, stacked high with cut grass and drawn by four enormous horses, was heading toward them. The stocky chestnut who was leading the horses hadn't noticed Stardust and Pippa, and at this rate Pippa knew they were all going to collide.

"Watch out, Stardust!" she screamed. "Cart to the left!"

Stardust turned her head, then slowed down in fright, unseating Pippa, who was forced to slide far up Stardust's neck.

"Sorry," Stardust said as she composed herself.

"Don't stop!" Pippa called, trying to push herself down Stardust's neck.

"But you might fall off," replied Stardust.

"I won't."

Gritting her teeth, Pippa clung on with all her strength. The ground raced by as Stardust's hooves carried them along at a frightening speed. If Pippa fell off now, Stardust might tread on her. Worse still, Pippa might even trip her friend up. She hung on tightly and pushed herself down Stardust's back. The cart was terrifyingly close.

"Out of the way!" Pippa screamed.

Frustration bubbled in her stomach. Couldn't the leading pony see the Night Mares and realize that they were chasing them? As they drew nearer, Pippa got a proper look at the leader. She recognized that square nose and those big eyes.

"Baroness Divine!"

The baroness didn't seem to notice the Night Mares and was smiling, apparently without a care in the world.

"What's she doing? Why is she here?" Stardust was confused. "She doesn't usually help with the harvest."

If they kept going, there would be a very nasty accident, so they had no

choice but to slow down. Snorting angrily, Stardust pawed the ground. They watched in frustration as the Night Mares galloped away.

"Afternoon," the baroness said, pulling up next to them. "My goodness, look at you both! Have you been having fun in the mud?"

Pippa eyed her suspiciously. It wasn't like the baroness to be so friendly.

"Yes, thank you, but we're too busy to stay and talk," Pippa replied.

Stardust darted behind the cart and broke into a gallop.

The Grasslands stretched ahead of them, flat and open, dotted with farm buildings, a forest in the distance. There was no sign of the Night Mares at all.

"They must be hiding," Stardust panted, dropping back to a canter. Her white coat was lathered with muddy sweat.

"Should I walk?" Pippa asked, running a hand down the pony's damp neck.

"I'm fine. We'll be quicker if you ride," Stardust said.

"Which way do you think they went?" Pippa asked as Stardust cantered on.

"It's got to be this way if they're going back to their home at the Volcano. We'll head toward the farm—it's the only place they can be hiding."

As the farm drew nearer, Stardust and Pippa whispered. Stardust placed her hooves carefully so that she was as quiet as possible.

"Over there," Pippa said suddenly,

"by the small barn—I saw something move."

Stardust switched direction. They'd almost reached the barn when there was a scuffling noise and the two Night Mares darted across the farmyard. One of them had the golden horseshoe in its mouth. Its eyes were wide with fear as it ran behind another barn.

"There!" called Stardust.

She chased after them but was too late—the Night Mares had disappeared.

Stardust stood very still, her ears swiveling as she tried to figure out where the Night Mares were hiding. Pippa listened too. At first all she could hear was her own heart pounding. Then a soft clatter grabbed her attention.

"Behind the grain store," she hissed.

Her stomach fluttered as Stardust went over to the building on hoof tips.

"Well, they're not here now," sighed Stardust.

Pippa stared in disbelief at the empty space. Some stones crunched behind her. Stardust turned around just in time for them to see the Night Mares run across the farmyard. The golden horse-shoe shone tantalizingly as they jumped over a fence and galloped away.

Chapter 6

"Hold on," said Stardust.

Pippa's hands shook as they cantered toward the fence. It was bigger than anything she'd jumped before. A shiver of fear ran down her spine. Stardust leaped at the jump. Just in time Pippa remembered to lift herself up off Stardust's back and grip with her knees. The wind whipped past her face and for a second she felt as if she was flying.

All her fears vanished—the jump felt fantastic. Then Stardust's front hooves hit the ground with a loud thud, and she raced after the Night Mares. The two scruffy ponies thundered on ahead, but they kept changing direction suddenly. Pippa quickly lost all sense of where she was. She was surprised when Stardust pulled up.

"Are you all right?" she asked.

"Yes," panted Stardust. "And I've had an idea. If we stop chasing the Night Mares, then they'll think we've given up and are heading home. I know another shortcut. I'm going to take it and hopefully we can cut them off."

"That's a brilliant idea," Pippa agreed.

Stardust waited for the Night Mares

to get totally out of sight so they wouldn't guess her plan. Once they'd disappeared, she headed into a nearby grove of trees. Pippa had to keep ducking her head to avoid being dragged off by low-hanging branches. Bushes and twigs snagged her legs as they hammered along the narrow path and jumped the fallen logs blocking their way. It was almost fun, but Pippa thought it didn't seem right to be enjoying the ride when there was so much at stake.

"Nearly there," Stardust called. "I just hope we've made it in time."

"Me too," said Pippa.

They burst out of the woods and into a clearing, where Trojan and a group of

ponies were lifting the newly harvested rectangular bales of grass from an open-topped cart and arranging them into an enormous haystack. There were snorts of alarm as Stardust pulled up, and work stopped immediately.

"What is going on?" A proud voice cut across the commotion.

"Crystal!" cried Stardust. Lowering her voice so that only Pippa could hear, she added, "I never thought I'd be so pleased to see her."

"Princess Stardust, why aren't you out in the fields picking up grass?" Crystal glared at her little sister and then at Pippa.

Stardust quickly explained how they had found two of the golden horseshoes and then how the Night Mares had stolen one back.

"I see," said Crystal. She took charge at once. "If the Night Mares see us here they'll run away, so everyone must hide in the trees. I'll wait behind this haystack and challenge them when they arrive. As next in line to the throne of

Chevalia, I'm sure they'll give me the horseshoe when I ask for it back—"

"But I thought—" interrupted Stardust.

Crystal gave her a steely glare. "Don't argue. I'm older than you."

"That's so typical of Crystal. We do all the hard work and she takes the glory," Stardust grumbled as she went to hide with the other ponies.

"It's very brave of her to challenge the Night Mares on her own," Pippa pointed out.

"Or stupid," Stardust said angrily. "Sometimes Crystal doesn't think things through. What happens if the Night Mares refuse to give her the horseshoe?"

"Then we're here to help," Pippa

replied, running a comforting hand down Stardust's neck. "She didn't tell *us* to stay hidden, did she?"

Stardust whinnied with laughter, then instantly fell silent as Trojan sent her a stern look and said, "Ssssh."

Pippa and Stardust hid in the trees a little distance from Trojan and waited. When the Night Mares didn't arrive, Pippa wondered if Stardust had been mistaken and they'd gone another way. She tried not to think about the three days left until Midsummer. If only the magic time bubble could stop time in Chevalia too! She'd stop it right now and only start it again when they'd found all the missing horseshoes.

Suddenly Stardust threw up her head. Her ears twitched, then swiveled to the right.

"Night Mares," she whispered softly.

In the distance Pippa could hear the drumming of hooves. She shivered with excitement. This was their chance to grab the golden horseshoe. They couldn't mess it up.

As the Night Mares ran closer, Pippa saw that they were being chased by a swarm of angry horseflies.

"You tricked ussss," buzzed the horse-flies. "Now give the golden horseshoe back to usss."

The Night Mares were scared. Their eyes were wild and their nostrils flared as they approached the clearing.

"Where's Crystal?" said Stardust. "She's supposed to challenge them. If she doesn't hurry up, it'll be too late."

"There she is." Pippa pointed as Crystal's head cautiously appeared around the side of the haystack, then quickly disappeared as she pulled back again.

"Oh no!" gasped Stardust. "I get it now. Crystal is scared of horseflies."

"Then it's up to us," Pippa replied.

Up close the Night Mares were frightening to look at, with wild eyes, straggly manes and tails, and bodies covered in gray volcanic ash. Stardust shook for just a moment before bravely stepping out of the woods and into their path.

"Stop!" she commanded. "Give the golden horseshoe back to us."

"Never!" the Night Mares shrieked, rearing up.

Stardust stood her ground as the Night Mares came closer, still pursued by the angry horseflies. Pippa was terrified that she and Stardust were about to be run down, and her knuckles whitened as she clutched Stardust's mane.

The Night Mares were so close that she could see the whites of their eyes and feel their hot breath flecked with spit. Her eyes watered at the bad smell that wafted toward her.

At the last moment the Night Mares neighed angrily, then changed course. In their hurry, one of them backed into Stardust, hitting Pippa's leg. Pippa winced but there was no time to examine the damage. The Night Mare with the horseshoe in its mouth was close enough for her to touch. Pippa reached out and grabbed it.

"No, it's mine," the Night Mare grunted, trying to tug it out of Pippa's grasp.

Pippa refused to let go, twisting her body so that she could keep hold of the horseshoe as Stardust turned around to kick into the air to scare the other Night Mare away. Pippa could feel herself slipping, but she held on tightly to the horseshoe, blinking back tears when a tail flicked in her eye.

The Night Mares shoved Stardust sideways. Pippa was dimly aware of Stardust grunting as she pushed them back and Crystal whinnying for everyone to stop. Stardust was barely holding her ground, until together the two Night Mares forced her toward the haystack. The horseflies buzzed angrily overhead.

Everything seemed to happen in slow motion. Pippa felt as if she was watching herself in a film as the haystack loomed right in front of her. There was an ominous creak, and then it was raining bales of hay. Pippa covered her head with her hands and gritted her teeth as she willed the avalanche to stop. But a hay bale whacked into Pippa and knocked her off Stardust. The next thing Pippa knew, she was being flung through the air.

Chapter 7

Pippa was lucky that she only fell onto a pile of hay rather than a hay bale. She lay on her back, grateful for such a soft landing, listening to the thundering hooves of the retreating Night Mares as the horseflies chased them away. A tall wall of rectangular hay bales towered above her—the only part of the haystack that remained. The rest of it littered the ground in messy clumps. She looked down at her hand and saw that she was still clutching the horseshoe.

"Look! I've still got the horseshoe," Pippa said, struggling up.

"Well done." Stardust had managed to stay upright, but she looked slightly dazed.

"Just look at the mess!" said Crystal,

who had narrowly missed being hit by the avalanche of hay. "We've been working on this haystack all day."

Pippa started to laugh—trust Crystal to worry about the mess when they'd just managed to rescue a horseshoe! She wrapped her arms around Stardust's hot neck.

"You were fantastic," Pippa said, hugging her.

"So were you," Stardust said proudly. "Mom and Dad are never going to believe us when we tell them what happened."

"They'll be absolutely thrilled!" said Pippa.

The ponies filed out of the woods led by Trojan. When they saw Pippa holding the golden horseshoe, their eyes widened and they whinnied excitedly.

"Are you all right?" Jet asked.

"What happened?" asked Comet.

"Pippa snatched it back from a Night Mare," boasted Stardust.

"Stardust and Crystal helped," Pippa said quickly.

Trojan sent Crystal such a look of admiration that it made her blush.

"Actually, I didn't do anything," she said. "It was all Stardust and Pippa's work."

Trojan was even more impressed that Crystal had been honest and not taken any of the credit, especially when it was offered to her. He softly brushed his nose against hers.

Crystal blushed so deeply that even the blaze on her apricot-colored face turned red. She shyly rubbed her nose against Trojan's, causing him to blush too.

"Aw! Sweet," Stardust whispered to her friend.

"Stop staring." Pippa giggled, pulling

her around. Every single one of Pippa's muscles ached, but she didn't care.

The horseflies returned, having chased the Night Mares far away.

"Thank you so much for all your help," said Crystal. "And I'm sorry I never took the time to listen to you before."

"Come back to the castle with us," Stardust said.

Zimb shook his head politely. "Our work isss done here," he buzzed, bowing low. "We're sssorry we caused you ssssso much trouble. In the future we will send a team of horsefliessss to guard the horseshoessss hanging on the ancient wall."

"Thank you," Stardust said gratefully.

"I'll have to ask Mom and Dad about it first, but it sounds like a brilliant idea."

The horseflies swarmed off, and Pippa, Stardust, Crystal, Trojan, and the princes walked back to the stream. By now the news had spread that two more horseshoes were safe, and as they walked through the Grasslands more ponies joined them.

Mucker was still guarding the other horseshoe and looked very impressed when Stardust and Pippa made their triumphant return.

"What happened to keeping clean?" he asked.

Stardust blushed prettily. "There's nothing wrong with a bit of muck and a good day's work," she answered. "We're taking the two horseshoes back to the castle to hang them on the ancient wall." Then she added, "In fact, everyone's invited."

An excited murmur rippled through the gathering of ponies. Cinders pushed herself to the front of the crowd.

"You can't appear in the Royal Court like that," she said. "Look how dirty you are! Give me the horseshoes. I'm clean—I'll take them back."

A cunning look flashed across her face, but it was gone so quickly that Pippa decided she must have imagined it.

"No, thanks," said Stardust. "Pippa and I did all the work. We're not letting you take the glory. We'll hang the horse-shoes ourselves."

"It's true—you *are* very dirty," said Crystal.

"We promise to be careful," Pippa said. "And we won't get the horseshoes muddy."

Crystal looked thoughtful. "Maybe it's time I lightened up a bit and was less proud and bossy."

She glanced at Trojan and a pink flush crept up her neck. Trojan was flushing too. Stardust nudged Pippa's arm and they giggled together. Crystal quickly recovered her composure.

"You can take the horseshoes back to the castle," Crystal said. "Then afterward I'm treating you both to a luxury session at the Mane Street Salon. You deserve some serious pampering. Pippa, ask for

the strawberry mane wash—I think you'll love it."

"Thank you," Pippa said. "That sounds wonderful."

Stardust turned to face the crowd. "So who's coming to the Royal Court with us?"

"Me! And me!" all of Canter's whinnied excitedly.

Side by side and both clutching a golden horseshoe, Pippa and Stardust led the procession back to Stableside Castle. Pippa's muscles still ached and she felt very tired, but extremely happy.

It took a while to get back and even longer for everyone to crowd into the ancient courtyard. All the prince and princess ponies lined up together to

watch. Queen Moonshine and King Firestar smiled proudly at Stardust and Pippa as they made their way to the Whispering Wall.

Cinders stood next to her mom, Baroness Divine, at the front of the crowd.

"There goes Princess Grunge," she said meanly.

Dipping her square face, the baroness whispered to Cinders, "The Royal Family has definitely lowered its standards."

Pippa didn't hear Cinders's answer but Baroness Divine chuckled quietly and whispered, "That's right, my dear. Things will soon be different in Chevalia."

The menace in her voice gave Pippa goose bumps. What did the baroness mean? But there was no time to think about it now. Reaching the queen, Pippa bowed her head and forced her aching legs into a low curtsy.

The queen lightly touched the top of Pippa's head with her nose. As Pippa stood up, she saw that there were tears in her beautiful dark eyes.

"Pippa MacDonald, you are truly a very special girl. You've worked hard today and weren't afraid to get your hands dirty. You were also very brave. Chevalia salutes you."

To Pippa's embarrassment, everyone cheered.

"Thank you, but I didn't do it on my own. Stardust helped, and the horseflies, and Mucker and Crystal," Pippa added generously.

"Hush, child," the queen said, smiling.

First Stardust and then Pippa handed a golden horseshoe to the king, who carefully hung them on the Whispering Wall. He stood back to admire them, and the crowd cheered again.

The wall didn't look so empty with four horseshoes hanging there, but Pippa was very conscious that time was running out. There were only three more days before Midsummer. Would they find all the missing horseshoes? The days ahead would be difficult and dangerous, but Pippa felt ready. Chevalia needed her more than ever.

"Congratulations," said Queen Moonshine. Then, as if echoing Pippa's thoughts, she added, "However, your quest isn't over. Midsummer Day will soon be here, and there are still four horseshoes to find. Go safely, my children, and please remember—don't count your horseshoes before they're hung!"

"Thank you, Your Majesty—and we won't," said Pippa.

Stardust reached out and nuzzled Pippa's arm.

"To Chevalia," she whispered.

"To Chevalia," Pippa replied softly.

Chevalia Now!

**EXCLUSIVE
INTERVIEW WITH
MUCKER**

by Tulip Inkhoof

There's no doubt that this Harvest Day will go down as the busiest one in Chevalia's history. Reporter Tulip Inkhoof caught up with Mucker, the youngest farm pony, for an eyewitness account of all today's action over in the Grasslands.

☆ **TI (Tulip Inkhoof):** Thanks for agreeing to speak to me, Mucker. May I just ask that you wash your horseshoes before we start the interview?

☆ **M (Mucker):** But I'm proud of my muddy hooves! Getting dirty and working hard are as much a part of Harvest Day as the picnic lunch.

2

☆ **TI:** Okay, and I understand that even the Royal Family enjoys mucking about on the farm?

☆ **M:** Stardust certainly does— she always helps out. In fact, she works so hard and gets so muddy that Cinders calls her Princess Grunge.

☆ **TI:** Was it a shock to learn that there were two golden horseshoes hidden in the grass?

☆ **M:** Yes, I couldn't believe it! The grass was growing really tall even though it hadn't rained, and we were beginning to wonder why. Thanks to Zimb and the horseflies, we discovered it was because of the magic from the golden horseshoes.

☆ **TI:** Talking horseflies indeed! Did you know they could communicate with you?

☆ **M:** I had no idea! I've batted away plenty of horseflies and never once did I think that they were trying to talk to me. It just goes to show that you don't truly understand someone until you've listened to them properly.

☆ **TI:** And I hear that the Night Mares stole a horseshoe almost as soon as it was discovered? How dramatic!

4

☆ **M:** Yes, Pippa and Stardust had just found the fourth missing horseshoe when two Night Mares came out of nowhere and snatched the horseshoe that Cinders was supposed to be guarding. Pippa gave me her horseshoe for safekeeping, then she and Stardust chased after the Night Mares.

5

They were so brave, and Trojan was really impressed with Crystal too!

☆ **TI:** Thanks for filling me in, Mucker. Now I suggest that you really do find a water trough and get cleaned up!

Will Pippa and Princess Stardust
find all the golden horseshoes?

DON'T MISS THEIR NEXT THREE
ADVENTURES IN CHEVALIA!

Turn the page to read a sneak peek . . .

Pippa woke with sunlight warming her face and the sound of singing in her ears. The music reminded her of her big sister, Miranda, who often sang in the mornings. Miranda was mostly out of tune though, unlike the beautiful voices Pippa could hear now. Curious, she got out of bed.

"Stardust, are you awake?"

Princess Stardust's straw blanket was crumpled as if she'd gotten up in a hurry.

A wave of homesickness hit Pippa as she stared around the empty room. Annoying as Miranda was, she missed her—and Mom and her little brother, Jack. Did they miss Pippa too?

Four days ago Pippa and her family had been on a beach vacation when two giant seahorses had taken her to the enchanted island of Chevalia, a world inhabited by talking ponies. Pippa had learned that Chevalia was in terrible danger. The eight golden horseshoes that gave the island life had been stolen from the Whispering Wall, an ancient courtyard wall in Stableside Castle. If the horseshoes weren't hanging back on the wall in time for Midsummer Day, their magical energy couldn't be renewed by the Midsummer sun and Chevalia would fade away. To Pippa's amazement, she had been asked to find the missing horseshoes. Along with her new best friend, a royal pony called Princess Stardust, she'd managed to find four of them, but Midsummer was three days away and there were still four horseshoes to find.

As Pippa got up, she remembered something important—Chevalia existed in a magical bubble. No time would pass in her world while she was on the island, meaning that none of her family would miss her. Pippa's homesickness vanished immediately.

She skipped to the window to see where the singing was coming from.

Princess Stardust's bedroom was in the smallest tower of the castle, topped with a pink flag, and it had a marvelous view. Pippa glanced at the sea sparkling in the distance before looking at the courtyard below.

"It's the Royal Court," she breathed.

All the ponies of the Royal Court were gathered together, with the princesses and princes in the front. Their colorful sashes and jeweled tiaras shimmered in the morning sun. Crystal, Stardust's bossy oldest sister, was conducting the singing with a riding crop, and the music made Pippa want to dance. When she had first arrived on Chevalia, Pippa had been so shy, but now she was starting to feel as if she belonged here and she couldn't wait to join them.

Pippa quickly put on the new outfit that had magically appeared overnight especially for her—a denim skirt, a striped T-shirt, leggings, and a sweat-shirt—then she hurried down the tower's spiral ramp.

"Excuse me," she whispered as she made her way to the front of the court-yard. The royal ponies smiled as they parted to let her through. "Thanks," she said.

Princess Honey was singing next to Stardust, tapping the ground in time to the music with a sparkly pink hoof. She was very pretty, with a shiny, straw-berry chestnut coat, but she couldn't

quite reach the higher notes, and her voice kept squeaking.

"You sound like a rusty stable door," Stardust said, laughing at her.

Honey hung her head.

"Hi, Stardust. Hi, Honey," Pippa whispered, squeezing between them. "What's going on?"

"We're rehearsing for the Royal Concert," Stardust replied. "We always hold it on Midsummer Day, to give thanks for Chevalia and the magical horseshoes. But Honey won't be allowed to sing if she keeps on making that racket." She playfully nudged her older sister.

Honey's brown eyes filled with tears. "You're so mean!" she said. Pushing past

Stardust, she trotted out of the court-yard.

"There isn't going to be a concert if we don't find the horseshoes," said Pippa. "But before we start searching for them, you'd better find Honey and say sorry for hurting her feelings."

Stardust was surprised. "I was only teasing. I didn't mean to upset her—I forgot how much she wanted to sing the solo."

Stardust was anxious to make it up to her sister, so together they sneaked out of the Royal Courtyard.

Once outside, she whinnied to Pippa, "Get on my back."

Pippa jumped onto Stardust's snowy white back, and they cantered off to look for Honey.

"There she is," Pippa said, pointing, as they left the castle over the drawbridge.

"She's heading for the Grasslands," Stardust said, galloping after her.

Leaning forward like a racing jockey, Pippa buried her fingers in Stardust's mane. The pony galloped so fast that the air rushed at Pippa's face, making her eyes water and her hair stream out behind her in dark, wavy ribbons.

Honey didn't stop at the Grasslands but galloped on across the Savannah.

"Where's she going?" Pippa shouted.

"I don't know." Stardust sounded worried. "This is the way to the Cloud Forest, but she can't be going there."

"Why not?"

Stardust's stride faltered slightly. "Because it's haunted."

Pippa tightened her fingers on Stardust's mane, knowing that if Honey entered the haunted forest, she and Stardust would have to follow her.

"Faster," Pippa urged.

Stardust lunged forward.

"Honey, wait!" called Pippa. "Stardust has something to say to you."

They were almost at the edge of the Cloud Forest when Stardust finally caught up with Honey.

"I'm sorry," Stardust panted. Her sides were heaving and Pippa slid from her back to give her a chance to catch her breath. "I didn't mean to hurt your feelings."

"I can't sing either," Pippa confided. "I'm useless at it, and I get so shy I blush."

"You, shy!" Stardust and Honey exclaimed together.

Pippa nodded. "I'm very shy about lots of things, but Mom says if you pretend to be confident, then everyone will think you are."

Stardust was impressed. "That's great advice! I never guessed that you were shy about anything."

Don't miss Pippa's journey to find the golden horseshoes and save Chevalia!